LIGHT OUT OF
BLUE DARKNESS

AMY PERRIN BROWN

authorHOUSE®

AuthorHouse™
1663 Liberty Drive
Bloomington, IN 47403
www.authorhouse.com
Phone: 833-262-8899

Published by AuthorHouse 06/13/2022

ISBN: 978-1-6655-6115-0 (sc)
ISBN: 978-1-6655-6113-6 (hc)
ISBN: 978-1-6655-6114-3 (e)

Library of Congress Control Number: 2022910215

Print information available on the last page.

Any people depicted in stock imagery provided by Getty Images are models, and such images are being used for illustrative purposes only. Certain stock imagery © Getty Images.

This book is printed on acid-free paper.

CONTENTS

CHAPTER 1

BIRTHDAY PARTY IN THE LIGHT

Mrs. Smith stood with her hands raised in praise of God. "Family, Family, Family. What a blessing. Oh my goodness! Look at this!"

Some who were related by blood and others related by love gathered around her. "How blessed we are to have family. I am so happy you all were able to come!" She returned to the kitchen shaking her head, thanking God and drying her eyes with the corner of her apron.

The large room glowed; a triple drape of pink and green flowered valances gave it an air of elegance. The sun shining through the picture window illuminated the gracious space as if every light were turned on. Old Sol, as she often called it, wrapped his reflection around a gold vase filled with a huge bouquet of tulips, yellow roses, and the filler, baby's breath.

In the center of the room, Rosie Maxwell, the guest of honor, sat as a queen in the wing-backed chair dwarfing her slender frame.

The room was filled with a group resembling the United Nations. Some had traveled from different parts of the country to celebrate the 90th birthday of the one they loved. There was no doubt about whom they were there to give tribute. Whether or not she knew who anyone was or why they were there could not be determined. Her mind had been snatched by the relentless disease Alzheimer's.

Everyone wanted to hug and kiss Rosie or just touch her to show their affection. She sat on the edge of the large chair, smiled, and rocked her body back and forth like she was in a rocking chair. She would clap her hands, laugh, or tap her feet to the symphony she heard in her head.

Unintelligible words came out of her mouth every now and then and she would chuckle as if hearing her own private joke. She welcomed all the attention she received on this day.

Multiple conversations were going on among the 35 people whom Kate had invited. About a third of the group was Rosie's extended family. The other two thirds were related to the Buchannan family who had employed Rosie for over thirty years. They all had stories of how Rosie was so important in their lives. They watched as Rosie's happy eyes circled the room, looking at each person, pausing at some longer than others, always smiling; maybe she was listening, understanding, or recalling the past.

Mrs. Smith wondered out loud, "I wish I could understand her words. I wonder what she's thinking. Do you think she remembers things, but just can't verbalize what's in her mind?"

As a smiling Mrs. Smith looked around the room to see if anyone needed anything, Sally Buchannan asked her, "That vase of flowers is so beautiful. I love the combination of the tulips, yellow roses, and baby's breath. Did you arrange them?"

"Those are Mrs. Maxwell's flowers. She has received a vase of flowers each and every week since she's been here. I thought Kate was sending them, but she said it wasn't her or her family. Maybe it's one of you...hmm." She looked around the room for a clue. No one confessed to being the benefactor, but everyone wished they had thought of being so benevolent.

"They arrive with a card that says only *LOVE/JOY*. Not knowing who they're from adds a little mystique to them. I'll tell you one thing, I look forward to their arrival. They make **her** happy too, but I try to keep her happy all the time, so she has no reason to be *blue.*"

Someone in the room yelled, "Wow, did you see that?"

"What? What is it, Bobby?"

Bobby's mouth was frozen open. "I... er...I don't know. Maybe it was my imagination."

Then some were saying, "No, I saw it too."

"What? What? What?," others murmured.

The ones who saw it all started talking at once. Those who were waiting for an answer could only make out one word.... *LIGHT....* .

"What are you saying? What did you see?"

Finally, as the room quieted down, Bobby said, "I don't know. Maybe it was the sun reflecting on Momma Rose's eyes, but for a second, it was like a bright light was shining *from* her eyes...a real bright light, and she looked like she was going to say something.I wonder, I wonder," he murmured as he stroked Momma Rose's cheek, "What is going on in her mind?"

CHAPTER 2

SASS AND SISTERS

Mardine yelled: "Yella Rose, Yella Rose! The more I say it, the madder she grows.

Hehehe.... Can't catch me... Can't catch me."

Twelve-year-old Mardine was hiding in the bushes just far enough away that Rosie could not tell exactly where the voice was coming from. Even though Rosie was a year older, Mardine usually started the fights. Mardine knew how to pull her chain. Rosie hated being called yellow. When she heard it, her blood started to boil, and she was ready for a fight.

"Yella Rose, Yella Rose, The more I say it, the madder she grows. Ha Ha Ha...... You can't catch me... Yella Rose." Mardine had reddish-brown skin like her mother, Anna, who was half Indian and half Negro. Mardine really didn't care that Rosie was "high yellow," the same color as her father, who had a white father and a negro mother. She just liked to tease, and Rosie was the only one who took the bait.

Anna and Daniel had 10 children, seven sons and three daughters. Five were Daniel's color, and five were Anna's color. Their difference in complexion was only an issue when Mardine wanted to irritate Rosie.

Mardine was hiding in the bushes that were off limits because of the poisonous red berries.

Rosie yelled to her, "I hope you eat some of those poison berries while you're in those bushes." Her plan was to make Mardine say something so she could determine just where she was hiding.

"Ouch", Rosie heard her sister's voice. She picked up a rock and threw it toward the sound.

"Missed by a mile, Yella Rose. I bet you're getting madder and madder, Yella Rose. She's mad... Yella Rose is MAAAAAD! Yella Rose is MAAAAAAD!!"

Mardine's taunting only made Rose madder. If she could only catch her, she would knock her down and punch her eyes out. "You won't be laughing when I catch you, MAGPIE MARDIE."

Anna Miller, or "Mama" as the kids called her, walked out the back door and saw Rose chasing Mardine through the yard. Usually, she let these episodes play out, but today she was preparing for her son, Brent, to take her and her children to town.

"Rosie!" she yelled from the back porch, "Go pick some collard greens for dinner. Mardine, get the bucket and heat up some water so you two can bathe before we go to town."

"Ah, Mama, how come I have to make a fire and heat up water, and all she has to do is pick greens?" Mardine whined.

Rose walked close enough to Mardine so only she could hear, but Anna could not, what she said under her breath, "Because you're so ugly, she's going to try to wash the ugly off of you, that's why."

Mardine threw the empty bucket at Rosie. She missed, but not by much. Anna shook her head and went back into the house.

CHAPTER 3

THE BLUE DRESS

The wagon rolled down the road making the dust and chickens scatter like swatted-at flies. The two older brothers of George Brent Miller had taught the fifteen-year-old how to handle the two-horse team like a professional driver. His long legs and arms helped.

Except for his height, Brent, as he was called, and Rosie could pass for twins. Maybe that was why Brent was Rosie's favorite brother, or it could be that he catered to her from the time she was born. He took care of her like she was a baby doll, always wanting to hold her or sing to her. As she grew, he would take her for walks. It was Brent who would rescue her when he could see Mardine teasing past the tolerance level. They would go to the wooded area behind the house and play games or throw rocks across the pond.

While they traveled the back roads, Mama, with her strong deep voice, led the singing of gospel songs, always starting with their favorite, *The Lord is Watching Over Me Right Now.* They sang for many reasons. Indeed, these roads were at some points very narrow so they wanted to warn anyone they might encounter that people were coming. Once, when they were going to town, the family saw a young couple on a blanket beside the road doing something they should be doing in their bedroom at home. Another time a polecat was startled by their singing; fortunately for them, they saw it as it turned and ran. The song also was a prayer asking God to watch over them in case the hooded ones were out to do harm.

As they neared town, with Anna sitting next to Brent, little brother John and sisters Annie, Mardine, and Rosie in the back, they talked quietly to each other. Annie was holding on to the pie that she had baked for Mrs. Washington who was ill.

First stop was the General Store for staples: flour, sugar, baking powder, soda, and vinegar. While Anna supervised Brent's placing of the goods in the wagon, Annie and Mardine took the 10-minute walk down the road to deliver the pie to Mrs. Washington who lived on the edge of town near the railroad track.

Rosie took John across the road to the dry goods store to wait for mother. Holding his small hand, she looked in the window and saw something that made her heart beat like a drum in a July 4th parade. It was a BLUE DRESS. It was the most beautiful blue dress that she ever laid her eyes upon. She was mesmerized by the sophisticated dress with puffy sleeves and a small white ruffle around the high neckline and the cuffs. Rosie stood and stared in the window, holding tightly to Little John's hand, with no idea how long she had been admiring the dress. In her mind, she heard music and saw herself smiling and dancing in circles, holding up the tail end of one side of the skirt.

She did not know she was humming aloud and unaware of the young boy who walked by and saw her staring. He looked up to see what had her attention. In a low voice he said, "You would look real pretty in that dress. "

"Who are you?" Rosie jumped as his words brought her out of her trance. She was unaware that he had been standing next to her until he spoke.

The tall, slim, handsome, brown-skinned youngster had large eyes and a beautiful smile. Blake smiled a huge grin, "They call me Lil Brother, but my name is Blake."

Just then Brent and Anna walked up to the two young people. Anna, frowning, but knowing Brent would handle the situation, brushed past them, and went into the store.

And he did handle it; "What you doing talking to my sister, boy?"

"She your sister? She sure is pretty." Blake could not wipe the smile off his face, but even though Brent was just a few years older, he respectfully kept his head down as he talked.

"She wants you to buy that dress for her."

Brent took a step back and looked the boy up and down, "How you know that, boy?"

"Cause she been standing there staring at it while you was loading your wagon."

Rosie was blushing at all this talk about her and in front of her, so she quickly left Brent and the boy talking, grabbed Little John's hand, and followed her mother into the store.

Anna was standing in the back of the store on the left side. This was the designated place where people of color had to wait. Mr. Ford had one white customer to wait on before he could acknowledge that she was in the store.

Mr. Ford had a lot of respect for the Miller family. There were some people in town who always wanted credit, but Anna Miller only bought what she could pay for at the time. She and her children entered the store clean, neat, and orderly. They knew their place and never stepped out of line. *There are some white folks who could take lessons from this family*, he thought. Mr. Ford could not let on that he felt that way, or the white folks would make trouble for him. So, he treated Anna Miller just like he treated the other negroes in the town.

"What you want today, Anna?"

She gave him the list, kept her eyes down, and stood back as Mr. Ford collected the items, assembled, totaled, and wrapped them in brown paper. Her children stood close to her so as not to suggest they were trying to steal anything. Rosie saw that blue dress on the rack in different sizes. As they left the store she drew attention to the beautiful blue dress.

"Mama, do you think we ever would have enough money for me to have my own *new* dress, like this one?"

Anna chuckled and asked her daughter, "Where you gonna wear a smart dress like that?"

"I could wear it to church like some of those girls that dress real nice."

"Girl, can you eat that dress? There are a whole lot of things this family needs to buy before we buy you a new dress for church."

Rosie's heart dropped. She had already visualized herself in that blue dress, and that boy said she would look pretty in it. *Who was that boy?* she thought. *What did he say his name was?* Why did it seem like she had seen him before? Oh well. . . .

Annie and Mardine joined them, so Rosie did not say another word about the blue dress. She had no desire to hear Mardine mocking her about something else. No use giving her a new thing to tease about. But on the ride home, she could not get that blue dress out of her mind. As the wagon rolled out of town, the family began to sing; that is, all except Rosie and Little John. He slept and all she could do was ruminate on that blue dress.

When they reached home and got out of the wagon Little John woke up and the first thing he said in a very loud voice, louder than he usually talked, was, "**Rosie got a boyfriend!**"

Oh no, please John, don't do this to me, she thought. She put her hand over his mouth trying to shut him up so Mardine would not hear him, but Mardine's ears lifted like a hound dog smelling a dead bird.

Little John was singing it like a song now, "Rosie's got a boyfriend… Rosie's got a boyfriend."

Brent, aware of what was going on, grabbed him, and offered him a ride on a tree to distract him. Mardine didn't say anything but tucked this information in her mind to use later.

That night after the dinner dishes were finished, Papa went out on the porch. Mardine was in Annie's room, and Mama, whose voice was usually deep, read the Bible in a soft, sweet register to the young boys. Rosie took this opportunity and eased her way out and sat beside Papa. Rosie thought she might try to work on him to buy that blue dress. On occasion Papa did buy pretty things for his daughters, though most of the time it was for Annie. It was worth a shot.

Papa was enjoying the cool breeze that was so rare on these hot nights. After the day's work in the fields getting everything ready for cotton picking, he just wanted to clear his mind and relax. Rosie eased up next to Papa. She sat for a minute without saying anything, thinking about how she would approach this situation.

"Are you tired, Papa?" Papa stretched and yawned and leaned back in his big porch chair filled with pillows that had the shape of his physique. Very seldom did anyone else sit in his chair. If you were in it and Papa was in plain sight, you knew to scurry out of it as fast as possible.

"Baby, I moved so many rocks today I could build a bridge to Alabama. I don't want nothing slowing us down once we start picking that cotton. It won't be long now. It looks like our cotton will be ready early, God willing, then others can help us pick, and we can help others pick. We gonna have a real good crop this year!"

She heard positive notes in his voice that led her to believe this was the right time to approach the blue dress purchase.

"Pa… papa," she stammered, "today while we were in town with Mama, I saw this dress in the dry goods store that was so beautiful. I never had a new dress of my own from the store. I- I- I was wondering if…if…we have a real good cotton crop…real good cotton crop…this year, you ….think….maybe…yo ….could……………buy me that dress?"

Whew! She got it out.

Papa was quiet. Seconds passed like hours before he spoke. "Baby, did you talk to your Mama about that dress?"

"Yeah, and she said we had to buy some other things first, but I just thought if we had a real good—a real good crop—like you just said we are going to have, maybe we would have enough money to buy that dress too." Words tumbled over each other as Rosie got her whole point across before Papa could speak.

Papa turned his whole body and looked at Rosie as if he were looking at an alien from out of space. "What's the matter with the dress you wear to church now? Why do you need a new, store-bought dress?"

Rosie continued to talk fast, and her voice was getting a little squeaky knowing she was treading on dangerous ground. Then she made a big mistake.

"But Papa, I never had my own new dress. Everything I wear is a hand-me-down from Annie. I just wanted my own new dress from the store."

In the light of the moon, Papa took another hard long look at Rosie. This time there was disgust in his eyes. Rosie knew, as soon as the name Annie came out of her mouth, that she had waded into forbidden waters.

Annie was Papa's favorite in the house. Sometimes the other kids called her "Queen Annie." Papa was always bringing her gifts big and small.

"MISSY!"

Rosie wondered, *What happened to Baby that he called me just a minute ago?*

"Who do you think you are that you are too good to wear hand-me-downs from your big sister?" Papa nearly roared at her.

Rosie knew she had lost the battle and folded her arms over her chest, stuck her bottom lip out, and started to pout.

Papa was still looking at her, "Missy…you better pull that lip in. We gonna worry about food on the table 'fore we go worrying about clothes on your back. We would have to have a huge cotton crop before we go buying extra stuff like that."

BAM! Selective hearing: To anyone else it would sound as if the chances of Rosie getting that blue dress were slim to none, but all Rosie heard Papa say was, "If we have a good crop I will buy the dress."

When she went back in the house, she saw Mardine bringing Little John out of Annie's room. Oh no! She knew that meant that Mardine had drilled him for the rest of the story. No surprise when Mardine whispered, "Rosie has a boyfriend."

Even that did not kill her spirit. Rosie went into her bedroom and twirled around as if she were already wearing the blue dress.

Every night afterwards, Rosie prayed and prayed for a good crop so she might get that dress. In her dreams she would see herself dancing around the room in the beautiful blue dress. She would yell at Mardine, "Look at Yella Rose now, Mardine...I have the blue dress and I am beautiful!" *Lord, Lord, please let this be a good cotton year. Lord, please let Papa buy that blue dress.*

God blessed Daniel Sampson Miller's crop that year. There was news of the boll weevil, the chief pest of the cotton growers, coming up from the south, wiping out whole cotton fields. *"Not this year 'ol boll weevil; not on this farm,"* he thought. Cotton growers in Mexico and Texas were devastated by the boll weevil, but Georgia was blessed with a good cotton season. It was extremely hot most of the summer. There was enough rain, but not too much. Because Papa had enough land, he could rotate crops and not take everything out of the soil...the cotton was good and abundant. It was the best crop they had had for many years.

The week before cotton-picking-time, Papa heard about a family that was trying to move north but didn't have enough money for the train ride. The Fenton family had twin eleven-year-old boys and two teenage girls, and the mom and dad and one five-year-old boy. This would be six extra people picking with the Miller family.

Papa made a proposition to them: "If you stay and help us pick cotton, you can stay here. I'll pay each one of you after all the cotton is picked."

"The Lord is watching over me right now." You could hear Papa singing this song in the field all day long.

Breakfast was served before sunrise so the crew could be ready to pick at first light. There was cornbread and pot liquor for lunch. The younger ones used small sacks and the big people used long sacks. The cotton grew tall, almost six feet.

Rosie, who usually had complained and whined about picking cotton because of pains in her legs, was up with Daniel early in the morning. Each day she did her best to pick more than anyone her age. She picked more than Mardine, which was a shock to everyone. At the end of the day her legs were sore and ached. Some days her mother told her to stay home, but she was determined to be a factor in this good cotton year. There was one thought going through her mind, the blue dress.

The only problem she had during the season was Mardine sneaking around Rosie's rows and whispering, "Rosie got a boyfriend." That soon stopped when Rosie told Mardine that one of the Fenton boys liked her. Mardine was afraid Rosie would start the "Mardine's got a boyfriend" talk, so she stopped bugging Rosie.

Many times during the picking season, Papa complimented Rosie on her hard work. "Baby, I am so proud of you," he said over and over. "You gonna get a good reward." Rosie had one reward on her mind, the blue dress.

Papa was so happy about the good year that the smile on his face never faded. It was there in the morning when he rolled out of bed before daybreak; it was there when he climbed into bed at night. Everything was going right. Every day you could hear him singing his own hymn of thanksgiving and laughing in the field, "Thank you Lord; thank you, Lord. Praise you, Lord, it's a beautiful day! I thank you Lord; what can I say? It's a beautiful day. Thank you, thank you, thank you!"

Papa and his crew were finished picking all his cotton early enough so his family and the Fenton family were able to help other farmers pick their cotton. It was a very profitable year.

The Fentons were paid and ready to leave. Anna packed enough food to hold them until they got out of the south. Everyone had boxes of their own fried chicken and biscuits. Before they left, Papa got everyone together to thank and praise the Lord. Mr. Fenton was anxious to leave, and he got a little nervous when Papa said he would pray. During the cotton picking season, he had watched his dinner turn from hot to cold many times while listening to Mr. Miller bless the food.

"Lord, we don't always thank you when we should. We don't always know why things happen, be they good or bad. But, Lord, on this day I want to thank you for all the good you have sent our way. Thank you for this family that had a stroke of bad luck and their bad luck was good luck for us. Thank you for this cotton and all the hands we had picking. Lord, I pray we don't forget that all things come from you and to you we must give back. Be with this family as they make a new life up north. And also Lord we also ask you to bless…".

At this point Mr. Fenton made a throat-clearing sound. Their family appreciated the Miller family and the send-off prayer, but they wanted to get on the road before the train left the station.

Papa got the hint and ended his prayer rather abruptly, "And bless the children. In the Lord's name we pray, Amen."

Brent eased the wagon out of the yard and onto the side road that would take them to the main road. The Fenton boys were waving and yelling thanks and goodbyes. Papa watched as they eased away, "We made some friends that we will have for life. I bet we haven't seen the last of them."

Mama and the kids were hoping he didn't mean they would be right back. Yes, maybe one day, but not right away. They were sad to see them go and happy to regain the space in the house. Anna always kept an eye on the boys around her teenage girls. And Mrs. Fenton had kept an eye on her daughters around the Miller boys. There was a lot to be learned while you were out picking cotton in the field all day, and it wasn't always a good education. Finally, the wagon was out of sight, and the dust was starting to settle.

The younger Miller boys immediately ran down to the creek to skip rocks across the water. They were so happy the hard work was over and there was time for play.

Rosie was going for a walk in the woods behind the house. She wanted to think about Papa going to town like he always did after the cotton-picking season. He would take some money and buy everyone a present. They all called it **Rewards Day**. She was walking and humming and thinking about the blue dress. Even though she wanted her family to make a good profit from the cotton, her mind had never veered away from that blue dress all through the long, hard, hot days of picking.

She heard Mardine calling her name and running behind her.

"OK. The Fentons are gone, you want to tell me about that boyfriend of yours."

Yes, the Fentons were gone now, and Mardine felt Rosie did not have a comeback. Rosie just ignored her and walked into the wooded part of the Miller acreage. "Oh, you don't want to talk about Little Brother?" Mardine wanted to brag on the information she pulled out of Little John weeks ago, before they picked cotton.

"Rosie's got a boyfriend, Rosie's got a boyfriend."

Rosie started to run, trying to get out of earshot of Mardine's annoying voice.

Mardine kept up, "Yella Rose and her boyfriend Black Little Brother."

Brent was out walking in the woods coming from the other way. Rosie ran into him with Mardine yelling behind her. He heard Mardine yelling, "Rosie got a boyfriend."

"Rosie, don't you know she just teases you because you react to her? Act like you don't care, and she'll stop."

"But I **do** care. It hurts my feelings when she calls me yella and talks about a boy that I don't even know, being my boyfriend."

"Come on now, Rosie, you're smarter than that. It's a game she's playing, and you fall into the trap every time. Grow up! Quit acting like a baby."

Brent, her favorite brother, had never talked to her like that. Now she was mad at him and Mardine. She wanted to go somewhere alone and cry.

"Come on, let's go for a walk. Come on Mardine, you want to walk with us."

Mardine joined them and they climbed up the hill. Rosie didn't talk as Brent and Mardine were laughing and having a good time.

"What do you think we'll get on Rewards Day?," Mardine wheedled. Brent tried to act like he didn't care. Rosie didn't answer. Mardine started rattling on about the candy she liked and hoped Papa would get her a big bag.

"What about you Rosie? What do you want?," Brent turned to her.

"Oh, I don't know. I hope it is a good surprise."

"Oh, I know what you want Rosie." Rosie held her breath. How could Mardine know about the blue dress? She shot Mardine a look filled with fear and rage.

"I know exactly what you want. I know. I know." Mardine ran ahead of Rosie and Brent.

"I know what you want Rosie. You want Little Brother to be your boyfriend. Rosie wants Little Brother to be her boyfriend." Mardine was jumping up and down and yelling thoroughly, enjoying her freedom once again, taunting Rosie.

Brent shot Rosie a look. She remembered what he said. She looked at Mardine and shouted back, "Yeah, I want Little Brother to be my boyfriend. Thanks Mardine, I'll tell Papa what I want."

Mardine felt outdone. "Oh, you can't fool me Rosie, I know you're acting like you don't care, but I know you do."

Rosie was so relieved that Mardine didn't know about the blue dress that she actually laughed. She ran the other way laughing and actually feeling pretty good. She thought, "Brent was right; all I have to do is pretend I don't care, even though I do."

Finally, the day came. Rewards Day. Papa went to town to buy gifts for everyone. Rosie spent most of the day watching for the dust to rise on the road signaling Papa's return. It was almost dinner time when she saw the wagon coming down the road. She ran out to meet Papa, cutting across the tomato garden and through the barnyard. Chickens scurried to get out of her way.

Papa stopped the wagon and let Rosie climb aboard for the short ride around the yard to the house. Rosie saw the brown-paper packages in the back of the wagon. One package was wrapped in the same brown color that Mr. Ford used in his store. In her heart she knew it was the blue dress. She peeked back and saw the bags of candy. Papa saw her sneaking a peek out the corner of his eye, "Alright, Baby, stop snooping around, you'll see what I got when everyone else sees."

Do you want me to help you carry everything in the house?" Rosie asked eagerly.

Daniel laughed at Rosie. "Baby, you sure are excited. Now go help

Mama get dinner on the table and we will open these gifts after dinner like we always do."

Dinner was way too long! While others chattered away, Rosie acted like she had been struck by lightning. She could hardly talk. Blue Dress, Blue Dress. It won't be long now. I will have that blue dress in my hands. I can smell it. I know it's in one of those packages. Papa kept talking about the stories he heard in town about the troubles other farmers had with their cotton pickers. Blue Dress, Blue Dress.

"Rosie, I said, do you want another biscuit? …..Rosie!"

"Oh, Oh, what?.. ..Oh no, thank you." *Blue Dress, Blue Dress.*

Then it was time. Papa gathered everyone together for rewards. The room got so quiet all they could hear was the crickets chirping. Father stood up, took a deep breath and said,

"Family, we had the best cotton crop we have ever had. We are more than blessed. Everyone bow your heads so we can thank the Lord." As Papa's prayer started the group was very still and quiet. Then as his prayer got longer and longer the family started to get antsy. Rosie was about to explode. The younger boys shuffled their feet and kept sighing. Little John went to sleep. Papa was unaware of anything but his solemn prayer of thanks for a good cotton crop. The prayer lasted an eternity for everyone except Papa. At long last Papa said, "Amen. Who is ready for their reward?"

Everyone yelled "Yes!" at once. Little John woke up. Papa laughed and called Brent first. He had a speech to go with each gift. "Brent, you are my right arm. You picked so much cotton I wanted to start calling you 'Cotton '." Everyone laughed.

"Truly Brent, I don't know what I would do without you."

Brent dropped his head as if he didn't know what to say. Papa reached back and brought out a shotgun. There was a mixed look of joy and sadness on Brent's face as he ran his hands down the barrel of the brand-new shiny shotgun. Tears ran down Brent's face. He thanked Papa and went over in the corner of the room to inspect his prize.

Next Papa gave the young boys their speech before he gave them each a bag of candy. Mama instructed them not to eat it all right away. They grabbed the bags and went out on the porch uninterested in what everyone else would receive. Then Papa had two identically sized packages wrapped in that brown-paper wrapping from Mr. Ford's store. He gave one to Rosie and one to Mardine.

Blue dress, blue dress, blue dress.…. It has to be, it has to be.… . Rosie and Mardine tore into the packages at the same time. As she ripped through the paper, Rosie saw a white blouse and one for Mardine, too. Identical white blouses were not anything Rosie wanted. She **never** wanted to dress like Mardine who was the bane of her misery.

As she was trying to control the tears that started down her cheeks, Papa picked up another package with that same brown wrapping and started walking her way. Ah ha, her mind was racing.….that's it, I get two gifts because I did such a good job picking cotton!

He stopped short. Mama was sitting in front of Rosie.

"I bet you forgot; good things come in small packages, Anna. For a wonderful wife." He reached into his pocket and gave her a small jewelry case. It was a beautiful cameo necklace. No one could remember Papa giving Mama jewelry. Anna cried and wiped the tears that rolled down her high cheekbones. This was a big surprise for her.

Papa still had the brown-wrapped package under his arms. The room was getting real hot. Rosie was almost soaking wet. Later, she remembered Mardine yelling with glee over the sparkling white blouse, but at the time Rosie was aware only of the package under Papa's arm.

Papa continued his walk toward Rosie. Her eyes were popping out of her head. She felt her head about to explode. Rosie thought about what Brent said about being teased. She thought her father was teasing her at this moment. What was really only seconds seemed like hours to Rosie as she watched Papa walk toward her. *Blue dress, blue dress, blue dress. Dear Lord, please let me see that blue dress,* she silently prayed!

And then her prayers were answered.

The blue dress she yearned for, the dress she had worked so hard for all summer picking cotton until her legs were about to fall off, the dress she dreamed of and asked her mother and father to buy her.…..That dress did appear in the room!

Papa walked toward Rosie, then right past her. In her excitement she was not aware that Annie was sitting behind her. Papa handed the package to Annie. When Annie opened the box and held up the blue dress she screamed for joy while Rosie yelled with pain. Her body felt like it was about to explode into a million little pieces. She felt hot and tingly all over. She felt her eyes roll to the back of her head, and then she passed out. This was the first time in her life that she fainted, but it would not be the last.

In the excitement no one realized what had happened. Mama was telling Papa how beautiful her necklace was while Annie jumped up and down screeching and grasping the blue dress and swishing it around. The boys ran in the house yelling because someone had dropped their candy and wanted the others to share.

When Brent noticed Rosie on the floor, even in the dim light, he could see she was colorless. He picked her up and everyone turned and looked at her. What happened? No one had an idea what was wrong with her. Anna got a wet cloth and put it on her forehead. Finally, Rosie started to come around. She looked up and everyone was standing over her looking down. Brent continued to hold her on his lap.

Everyone was asking her at once, "What's wrong? What happened?"

She was physically and mentally in pain. Her whole body ached. Her head was spinning. How could Papa do this to her? It was bad enough that he did not buy her the dress, but to buy it for Annie? Why, why, why??? Why was everyone so mean?

Rosie got up and told the group she was alright. "I think I'm going to lie down." In a low solemn voice she thanked Papa for the blouse, and she left the room.

In her room she put the pillow over her head and cried and cried until she used up all her tears. She was hurting and, in her mind, she kept asking *Why?* over and over again. *One day*, she thought, *I will have my own fine clothes. One day I will buy me a new dress just like I like.* With the pillow over her head, she eventually went to sleep. When Mardine came into the room, she was oblivious to what was going on with her sister.

Before Mama went to bed that night, she peeked in on Rosie. She sat on the side of the bed and put her hand on her daughter's forehead to check for a fever. "Are you OK, Rosie?" she whispered so as not to wake Mardine. Rosie did not answer, and Mama knew that she was pretending to be asleep.

Anna lay in her bed and thought about all the things that happened that night. She was worried about her daughter fainting on such a happy occasion. She was trying to figure out what could be the problem. Was something physically wrong? In the back of her mind there was something that she could not recall. She lay awake trying to dig back through the last few days and weeks. Hours passed.

Lord knows she loved all her children, but this cotton-picking time had been so stressful on the whole family, especially with seven additional people living in the house. She didn't mean to neglect anyone. Were there any signs that Rosie was sick during the last month or so? She remembered the times Rosie could hardly walk but insisted on going out to help pick.

After thinking about it, Anna remembered that Rosie had acted reserved and quiet all through the cotton picking. With all the people in the house it's hard to tell what was going on. *The last time we had talked more than two words to each other was in the dry goods store,* she thought.

*That's it! It happened **before** the cotton picking, before all the people were living in the house, before they knew the crop would be the best ever.... Rosie had asked for the same dress that Papa gave to Annie.*

This explained everything. That's why Rosie was so agreeable to pick cotton and why Rosie was so quiet most of the time. Rosie had her hopes set on that same blue dress. It was bad enough that she didn't get it for herself, but Papa had bought it for her big sister. Papa had a habit of spoiling Annie, in his attempt to make up for his first daughter, who died when she was three years old.

The next afternoon Mama talked to him about what came to her mind, "You love us all, Daniel, and you're good to me and the children. But don't you think sometimes you give too much to Annie and not enough to the others?" Her voice was gentle and low.

Papa's eyes turned red, and he looked at Mama with a mean, angry look. His voice was loud and gruff, "Woman, don't ever tell me what to do or buy for any of my children again—and I mean that. I will show favor to who I want to show favor."

Mama said no more about it.

The berries on the bush behind the house were red and poisonous. Often, Mama had warned the children never to eat or pick them, "They will make you terribly sick or kill you. And they will stain your clothes!"

The first time Annie picked up the blue dress to wear, the pockets held a bunch of those berries. The dress was permanently stained. When Annie discovered the damaged dress, she showed Mama. Annie had no idea why the berries were in the pocket or who put them there, but Mama knew instantly who did it and why.

Anna sat her oldest daughter down and explained to her the story behind the blue dress. "There is more to the dress than you know, my child. Rosie saw that same dress in the dry goods store when we went to town. She had her heart set on that dress before cotton picking time. We should have known there was a reason she drug herself out there to pick cotton like a mad person."

"Annie, you know your father gives you more than all the other children, but I don't know if you know why. Before your Papa and I were married, he was married to someone else. He and his first wife had a beautiful daughter whom he loved so much. His wife died while giving birth to their second child. With the help of neighbors and relatives he took special care of his daughter. Then one day she died also. His heart was broken. So, Annie, when you were born, he poured all the love he had for his first family onto you."

"The boys and Mardine don't notice this, but Rosie feels neglected by all the favoritism he shows to you. I ask you to forgive your sister for her act of jealousy. Don't talk about it. This situation will work itself out."

Annie wiped her tears and gave her mother a hug; she understood. Because she was a gentle soul like her mother, she never mentioned the dress again.

Sunday morning when Annie came to breakfast, Papa asked her why she wasn't wearing her new dress to church. Annie told him the dress was stained, and he asked to see it. His deep set eyes went from the dress to his second daughter. There was no discussion. He knew who did it, but he did not know why.

"I want to see you behind the shed after church," he said to Rosie.

Ordinarily the thought of a spanking by Papa, which almost never happened, would put the fear of God into Rosie. That day her pain was so deep she almost welcomed the beating she knew she had been promised. After church as soon as the wagon stopped in front of the house, Rosie marched right to the shed. She accepted her spanking without resistance. She did not cry, flinch, or oppose the spanking in any way. Papa was more upset than she was after the spanking. Since she did not react, he tried to do something else that he thought might upset her, "Go get that blouse I gave you, so I can give it to Annie." He was sure this would teach her a lesson about being mean. But Rosie was happy to get the blouse and give it to Papa. If Papa had asked Mama's advice, she would have told him Rosie did not want to go anywhere dressed like Mardine; he did her a favor. Besides, her mind was still set on one day having a beautiful new blue dress of her own.

Sunday night Rosie did not sleep. When morning came, she was up early doing her chores with a deliberate, angry attitude. Her eyes were red, and her face drawn as she joined the family for breakfast. Mostly looking down, she avoided eye contact with everyone. She had made up her mind during the long sleepless night to ignore the inevitable taunts from Mardine. The pain was like a knife slicing through her whole body; from toes to head. The words kept repeating themselves in her mind. *How could Papa be so mean?* How could he buy the dress that she wanted so badly and then give it to Annie? *He said if the crop was good that he might consider buying ME the dress, not Annie. He bought everything for Annie.*

Though the anger filled her body, she was not mad at Annie. Her big sister was sweet, kind, and loving. Annie apologized to her younger sister after the spanking. She would have given Rosie the dress if Papa would not object. She shared everything with her younger sisters. Often Rosie heard Annie tell Mardine to stop the teasing.

It was not Annie, but Papa. *Why? Why? Why? Does he hate me that much?*

Rosie did not realize that Papa had forgotten the whole conversation that he had with her about the blue dress. He had been so intent on getting the cotton picked and sold that anything happening before the picking was gone from his mind. He ate, slept, and worried about the cotton crop. Beyond that, he gave little thought to the world around him. On Reward Day when he walked into the dry goods store, he asked Mr. Ford to pick out something real nice for Annie and his two other daughters. He really liked the blue dress when Mr. Ford picked it out. Maybe in the back of his mind, he remembered that the blue dress was there, but he always bought Annie's present first. He had spent more money than he had planned, but he was so happy with the successful cotton season that he wanted to please everyone.

The episode with Rosie changed his joy to anger. His wife telling him what to do just added fuel to the fire. Daniel was the man of his house, and nobody would order him around. Nobody! What Rosie did was downright evil. She would not have her way in his household.

Anna, on the other hand, felt her daughter's pain. She watched Rosie as she moped around the house doing her chores. When she was finished, she went to her room and lay on the bed until dinner time. She ate dinner, did her chores, and went back to her room. Even Mardine's chants and teasing didn't upset her or cause any reaction.

CHAPTER 4

THE STORM

The storm clashed with thunder and lightning. Wind tore at the house and shot paper through the yard. The family had to make sure everything was inside and tied down. Papa told everyone to go to bed, and he would call them if they needed to go down in the storage room or the back room. Thumping on the house kept everyone awake and full of fear.

As he looked at the wild weather outside, Papa thought about how happy he was that the family had picked all their cotton, sold it, and received the money. There were many other farmers who were struggling to get everything done, cotton picked, and more. Elsewhere in the house, Mardine slept like nothing was going on. Rosie, on the other hand, was able to doze off only for a few minutes, but mostly she was wide awake thinking about one thing that she couldn't get out of her mind...*the blue dress*.

When dawn broke and the rain had stopped, Rosie was the first one up. She was standing on the back porch when Papa came out barely noticing her. Like all the other farmers, Papa went out to examine the houses, farm, and fence.

Soon the whole family was in the yard to see how much damage had been done. Brent ate a quick breakfast, then took his wheelbarrow and went to the wooded area to collect broken trees. He had to move fast or others would collect them for firewood as if it were on their land. Not many trees were down, so he was able to pick up what he saw and then get the limbs to the barn. He was worried about the tree with holes where he kept his artwork. Papa did not like Brent drawing. That was simply not what men do. Brent loved drawing and artwork. The wooded area was his hiding place to do what he enjoyed. He would draw pictures then hide them in the hollow tree.

Next to his ART TREE was a tree he had always liked…not too big, just a pretty tree. It was lying almost all the way down. He was sure he could set it up and pack some dirt around the trunk to save it. He was happy that he brought the shovel and the saw. He reached a little deeper to dig the hole when he saw something in the ground by the roots of the tree. As he dug a little deeper, the shovel hit something hard. He removed more dirt and saw a box or something under the roots. He dug around and realized it was a heavy case. He worked at it a while and finally got it out. Quickly he put the case in the wheelbarrow and covered it with branches and leaves. After he sawed off a few branches and stomped through the mud and other tree branches, he took the box to the barn and hid it in the corner under the hay.

In the back of his mind, something said, *Don't open it*. He wanted so badly to open the case, but his hands trembled when he started to walk toward it. He turned around suddenly and saw Rosie quietly standing there looking at him. She was still upset. Still about that blue dress.

Brent did not want to talk to her. Rosie stood there for about five minutes while Brent was loading wood over the hay. He thought, *I don't want to share this with anybody, whatever it is. Maybe there's money in the box I could use to get away from the farm. I could get myself to a place where I could live and draw in peace.* He had thought often about moving to Cleveland with his brother, but he knew his parents needed him here.

When he turned around, his sister was gone. He didn't know if she'd seen the box or not. He checked outside if anyone was coming. There was a hole in another corner where he used to hide things. He put the box in the hole and packed dirt around it. Then reluctantly, he went back to the wooded area. *What else am I going to find?* he wondered.

He returned to the tree he had restored to its upright position. It looked as if it had never fallen. He loaded the wagon again and was ready to leave, when, just as he thought would happen, a white guy on horseback rode in looking for wood. When he saw Brent, he turned away.

Several thoughts came to Brent about the white man wandering around on his land. Did *the white man know about the box? Why would he know about something on our land? Who was he?*

Later, he would learn answers to several of those questions.

Days later, Mr. Miller, the neighbor who had the same last name as the family, came over and asked Daniel if Brent could ride with him to Cleveland to pick up some furniture. Brent was in the barn wishing he could go somewhere and do his artwork. He was pushing the younger boys to do some work. *Even the girls could do some more work around here,* he thought.

From inside the barn, he heard Mr. Miller talking with Papa, "It would only take a couple of days, Daniel, and I'll pay him."

Brent was listening inside the barn and feeling happy. He said to himself in a large voice, *YES…YES…YES..LET ME GO….PLEASE!*

Papa was not happy to let his son go; he depended on Brent around the farm. But he knew it was about time to let Brent grow up a bit more. Papa told Mama and they agreed. Later, Brent went to the barn while everyone else was at dinner. He wanted to make sure all his stuff was still well hidden. Once, a while ago, he had caught the younger ones looking around in his stuff. Another time, the boys had seen Brent placing a box in another box. Now, Rosie was watching him move a large box into the barn. She never found out what it was or what he did with the box. She didn't look back to see.

Several nights later, when he was sure he was alone, Brent pried his way into the box. He was shocked to see more money than he had ever seen in one place. At first, he thought to himself, *This money can help me finally realize my dream! I'm getting the heck up out of here! I'm gonna finally get to be the artist I always wanted!* Brent decided to keep this secret for now, because he didn't want anything to stop him from living the life of his dreams.

Later that summer, Anna sent Brent to their cousin Lance's house with some food and staples. Lance's wife had just had her second baby. Brent informed his mother that his sister-in-law had fallen and twisted her ankle so she could not walk on it. She was having a hard time getting around with that little one running all over the place and a new baby.

Mama instantly called Rosie, "Pack a bag, child, and go with Brent down to Lance's place to help Mabel with the baby. You will probably be there until school starts. Help her as much as you can in the next two weeks."

Sitting next to Brent on the ride down the road, Rosie tried to shake her sadness. This was an opportunity to get away from the family and think about something other than not getting the blue dress and ruining the blue dress. At first, Brent didn't try to talk.

Passing the big tree right before Lance's road, Brent turned to his sister and said, "Rosie, you know what you did was wrong." Rosie's head dropped and she felt a dark cloud cover her whole body. Her heart started a faster beat. The one person she hated to disappoint was Brent. She could not look at him.

"Sometimes in life things just don't work out the way we think they should, but that does not mean we can take revenge on our own." Brent's voice hoarsened and sounded ready to crack. "You're not the only one wanting something you can't have."

Rosie stole a peek at Brent because it seemed he was talking about something other than the blue dress. He had a big frown on his face, his forehead was wrinkled. As fast as that thought came to her, Brent continued, "Papa thought he was making everyone happy, and he was happy."

His tone of voice was rougher and louder than Rosie ever heard him speak. "Do you ever think of anyone but yourself? Do you know how much money you wasted? Can you imagine how bad he must have felt when you destroyed that dress? You probably didn't even apologize to Papa and Annie. "

Rosie didn't move or answer.

Brent turned and looked at her, "Well, did you?"

Rosie just shook her head no.

Brent let out a disgusted sigh. The thick dark cloud clung to her. Brent had never talked like this to her. She thought, "What's wrong with him?"

He stopped the horses and told her to get down. He didn't say goodbye or help her with her bag. Rosie didn't see the tears in his eyes as he turned the horses and went back down the road.

CHAPTER 5

Taking Care of Family

Walking into Lance's yard, the first thing Rosie noticed was that it needed to be swept. She knew she was there to babysit, but she would spruce up this place before she left. Rosie walked to the porch and yelled through the screen door, "Anybody home?" The first thing she heard was the patter of little feet running to the door. Then they heard Mabel yelling at her two-year-old son not to open the door.

Rosie was a natural with babies and young children. She long had cared for her little brother John who barely had made it into this world. Born sickly, he suffered one ailment after another. While the other boys ran and played, John didn't have strength to keep up. Rosie would read, sing, and play with him to keep him happy. She would miss Little John while she was at Lance's, and was glad there were children here.

Rosie asked Mabel if she could clean and cook while she was there. Mabel couldn't be more pleased. Rosie fixed dinner, cleaned the house, swept the yard, and took the baby after Mabel nursed him. Mabel could not believe how organized she was. That evening after dinner Rosie took the baby out to the porch while Mabel gave the toddler a bath, the one thing she could do while sitting.

While relaxing on the porch, humming a lullaby, she heard someone say "Hey."

Rosie jumped and almost dropped the baby, because she hadn't heard anyone approaching.

"You gonna jump every time you see me?" he asked. She recognized the boy as the one who was talking to her outside the dry goods store.

Doggone it! She was trying to forget about that blue dress and things kept bringing it back. "Who are you? And where did you come from?" she blurted.

"My name is Blake, but people call me Lil Brother," he said looking down at the ground, "and I live down the road. I came to see my cousin."

"Who's your cousin?"

"You're holding him."

"This is not your cousin; this is my cousin." Rosie was defiant, if confused.

"Well, he's my cousin too."

Rosie heard Mabel calling from inside the house, "Lil Brother is that you, na?" Mabel had a habit of saying "na" at the end of each sentence. "Come in here and give your auntie a kiss, na."

Blake walked past Rosie going into the house, saying in a low voice, "Girl, you sure are hard to talk to."

Blake was a handsome, shy teenager. He was tall for his age and when he talked, he looked down at the ground, not making eye contact. His voice was always calm and pleasant. After a few minutes, Mabel came out on the porch leaning on Blake. He helped her sit down on one side of Rosie and he sat on the other.

"So Rosie, you met my sister's son-na. I believe you two are about the same age-na. How old are you, Rosie-na?"

"Help me back into the house, boy, I want to show you something-na. Come with us Rosie-na." Inside she instructed Lil Brother to hand her a box off the top of the shelf. Dust flew down as he lowered it to the table Rosie knew where she would clean tomorrow.

"Here's a picture of him when he was a baby-na. That man came around taking pictures-na." She handed Rosie a picture of a beautiful, big-eyed, curly head, naked baby. "Ain't he pretty-na?"

"NO, Aunt Mabel, don't show those naked pictures." Blake was protesting as Mabel handed the pictures to Rosie.

Rosie laughed as she watched the young man blush and scramble to hide the picture of his nude anatomy.

"I wish that man would come and take pictures of my babies-na."

"I hope that man don't come, so my cousins don't have to worry about you showing them to everyone when they grow up." Everyone laughed.

By the time Lance came back from doing the chores, the small group had had an enjoyable visit. Rosie, without realizing it, felt happiness for the first time in weeks. The baby was starting to cry for another nursing, so Rosie and Blake went back out to the porch.

"I remember seeing you in front of the dry goods store looking at that dress."

The color left Rosie's face as she thought about the blue dress again, "I guess that's never going out of my mind."

Blake saw the change in her demeanor and said, "Wow, what did I say?"

Rosie fought through her sadness and tried to change the subject. Regrouping she asked, "Why were you in town that day?"

"I was just getting off from work. I help out at the feed store."

There was a long silence. Rosie could not stop thinking of the blue dress and all the stress it had caused in her life, and Blake was trying not to look at a very pretty girl.

Finally, he said, "Well, I better get out of here; it's going to be dark soon. He hollered through the door, "Bye, Uncle Lance. Bye, Aunt Mabel. I gotta get on down the road." He heard them both shout goodbye.

How long you going to be here, Pretty Rosie?"

Rosie's head jumped around when he called her *Pretty*. No one had ever said that to her before. The thought went through her head of Little John saying, "Rosie got a boyfriend." It kind of scared her. She felt the fluttery rise of that fight-or-flight feeling.

"You go into your own thoughts a lot," he said.

Fighting for words to try to change the subject, Rosie asked, "How come I never saw you at school?"

"Because I go to Ballard in town. I stay there through the week and come home on weekends. See you later, Pretty Rosie."

He turned at the tree and disappeared as quietly and quickly as he appeared. Rosie felt a surge go through her body that she never remembered feeling before. He called her pretty.

I like Pretty Rosie much better than Yella Rose, she thought. *I wonder if*

I will ever see him again? Sitting on the porch Rosie felt good. She realized she had laughed for the first time in weeks. There was no Mardine to tease her, and she liked the attention from Blake.

Blake did not come back the next day. The only reason he didn't was he didn't want to seem overanxious. When he did come back, Rosie was on the porch with the two children. Blake came up and started playing with the toddler. Blake and the toddler ran and played in the yard as Rosie followed them around with the baby.

Rosie got to know and like Blake. She worked hard during the day cleaning and cooking for Mabel. By the time her two weeks were up she had cleaned every cupboard, washed every dish, washed the walls, washed and sorted all the clothes in the house, fixed dinners, and swept the yard. Mabel, who was not the best of housekeepers, learned a lot from her niece in the two weeks she was there. Mabel hated to see the time come when Rosie would leave.

Blake came every other day after the first week, then every day. By the third visit he was bringing little gifts. The first day he brought a coral-colored rock. One day he brought a large apple from the tree in his yard. The next time he brought pecans that he had shelled and wrapped in brown paper. The two young people sat on the porch and ate them before he went home.

One day while they were talking, he asked her about her family.

Rosie explained, "I have seven brothers and two sisters. One sister I love and one I can't stand.

Blake looked confused, "I can't imagine having a family member that I don't like. What if something happened to her, how would you feel?" Rosie could not answer, which made him more perplexed, "Family is all you have. How could you not love your sister?"

Rosie did not want to go into the teasing and name-calling she had endured all her life. She was still working on trying to ignore Mardine. She tried to substantiate her statement, "My sister is just plain mean; she does not treat me like a sister. We will never get along."

"You're so lucky to have such a large family. It's just me and my sister and she is older. She is getting married soon. I sure will miss her if she moves."

The last day before Rosie was to leave, Blake came and brought her a rose. Not realizing the couple's relationship, Lance came up from the field covered in dirt and asked Blake to come away and give him a hand, "Lil Brother," he said breathing heavily, "I'm sure glad to see you! I need some help moving a few big rocks from a piece of land I want to clear for next year's planting. I been working on it a lot, but another set of hands can help me finish."

Of course, Blake agreed to help, but he uncharacteristically kept his eyes glued on Rosie as he walked away. They were both upset that on their last day they would not get a chance to spend time together.

When Blake finished helping Lance, he came back to the house to say goodbye. Rosie walked him to the edge of the yard. Looking down, Blake pushed an acorn around with the toe of his shoe. He was hesitant about what he was about to say. It seemed like he was trying to get something in order before he spit it out. Finally, he said, "When I see you again, I hope you and your sister will be better friends."

"First of all," she said in a voice that was bordering on sassy, "Why do you think I will ever see you again and why is it important to you what goes on between me and my sister?"

He looked straight into her eyes and said, "Everything you do is important to me because when we grow up, we are going to get married." Then with a wink he said, "Bye, Pretty Rosie." He disappeared down the road.

Months passed before she saw Blake again, but she never stopped thinking about his last words: ". . .because when we grow up, I'm going to marry you, Pretty Rosie." She looked for him the few times she was able to go into town. The feed store was around the corner, but she was not allowed to walk down there alone.

Summer, fall, winter and then spring again. During all that time, she thought of him often. Mardine still teased, but not as much because Rosie paid her little or no attention. Time went on. She never forgot the blue dress. It came to mind whenever she thought about Blake.

In the spring of that year, came the annual church picnic. The Baptist, Primitive Baptist, AME, CME, and other churches from around the area would gather at one spot for a sermon and dinner. There would be lots of fried chicken, ice cream, layered cakes, lemon, apple, pecan, and sweet potato pies.

The ceremony started with a gospel choir from one of the churches. Harmonious voices floated over the emerald-green terrain bursting with flowers open to welcome spring and the picnic. A man's solo voice began rising above all the others. Rosie's heart began to beat as she recognized the voice: Blake.

"OH HHHH, Faaather don't leeeave mee. You have promised your hand would keeeeep meee........"

His voice was beautiful. All the background noise of children and old ladies murmuring and talking ceased. Blake sang and everyone listened. The choir joined in, and then the song was over. Folks rose to a standing ovation, something that very seldom happened at a church gathering.

After the singing and a long, drawn-out southern-style sermon, the people gathered to eat. As long lines formed, Rosie told Mama she was going to look for Aunt Mabel and Uncle Lance. She thought maybe if she could get close to them, she might see Blake. She wandered down the hill close to the area where the choir was singing. She stood with her hands over her eyes to shield the sun, searching, looking over the hundreds of people trying to find Blake.

She heard the mellow voice behind her, "Hello, Pretty Rosie." Before she could catch herself, she jumped.

"I guess you *are* going to jump every time you see me." His smile made him more handsome. He was taller than he was last year. "Looking for someone?"

Rosie wished she could control the heartbeat. She was sure he could see and hear the thump, thump, thump. She tried to keep her composure. "Oh, hi, Blake, how are you?," she said coolly.

Before he could answer, four young girls ran up to him to congratulate him on the good job he did with his solo. "We don't know you, but we want to tell you how much we enjoyed your song. It was great." The four girls were still talking when another group of people crowded around him to praise his praising. Rosie was pushed back away from Blake. She decided to walk away.

Blake was thanking the people, but he watched which way Rosie was walking. Finally, he told his admirers he had to go and he ran to catch up with her. Quietly he said, "Is that how you're going to do when we get married?"

Rosie couldn't speak. So infatuated was she with this young man, that the cat took her tongue. Finally, words came, "Your fan club is right. Your solo was fantastic. Did you hear the people on the hill screaming when you finished singing?

"OK, enough about my singing! How are you? Have you been keeping anybody's babies lately?" Before long they were laughing and talking like two old friends. Then he had to bring up Mardine, "How are you getting along with your sister?"

"Actually, we're getting along better. I've learned to ignore her, and that upsets her, so she leaves me alone. It all works out, " she grinned.

To change the subject, Rosie asked him how his sister was doing. "Did she get married and move away?"

Rosie could see the hurt in his eyes when he told her she had moved to Detroit. "I miss her so much. I sure will be happy when we get married in four years."

Rosie turned red all over. She felt the thrill going through her body.

Out of nowhere Mardine appeared. Looking like someone interviewing a client for a job, Mardine cased Blake up and down. Slowly–still looking– she said, "Rosie, Mama is looking for you. And, who is this boy?"

Blake was very polite to Mardine as he introduced himself, but gave no details. Mardine did not know he was the boy who had sung the solo. Calmly, Rosie asked Mardine to tell Mama she would be right there. She wanted Mardine to leave. Mardine grabbed her sister's hand and tried to lead her to the family picnic spot.

"I have to pick up something from Aunt Mabel. I'll be right there." Mardine was insistent on staying with Rosie until Brent came up behind her. Grabbing Mardine's arm, he demanded that she be his partner in the sock race. He spun Mardine away in one direction while Rosie and Blake, laughing, hurried off in the other.

The young couple never heard the dinner bell ring. They never saw the four-layer coconut cake that won the best cake contest. They didn't smell the chicken cooking on the open fire spit. They did see the *ever* in the evergreen trees. They smelled the honey in the honeysuckle vine. They saw two lovebirds cooing on a branch as surely as if they were looking in a mirror. Their silent walk-away from the crowd was romantic without a word or touch. Rosie was afraid to look at Blake because her heart was playing a drum roll that might get loud enough for him to hear.

Finally, she broke the silence asking him, "My, where did you learn how to sing?"

"I could carry a tune before I went to Ballard school, but they taught me what to do with my voice. It is a really good school. I am blessed to be able to go there. The music teacher is excellent."

"I wish I could go there. How do you get in?"

"My parents told them about my singing, and they recruited me."

"So much for that, then. I can't sing."

"They have all kinds of programs; you'd love it. What do you want to be when you grow up? Other than my wife, that is."

Rosie blushed and just as she started to say something he added the "my wife" statement, and she lost her voice again. She regrouped and her voice started to work, "...uh...uh...a nurse or a teacher. I like working with young children."

"They have a teachers' program there. You know, you must live in town all week. Sure you wouldn't miss your family too much?" he teased. "Oh, by the way, was that the sister you love or the sister who gets on your nerves?"

They laughed. He knew by the way Mardine was tugging on Rosie which sister it was. They started walking back to the crowd, passing other young people trying to have their moment of solitude. I better see what my Mama wants. How long have we been gone?"

"I'll see you again, Rosie. They can't keep us apart." He held her hand and said, "Goodbye wife-to-be," and walked away.

Rosie found her way back to the family picnic table. "Mama, I'm sorry for taking so long to get here," she said quickly and a little out of breath.

Mama looked up from talking with Annie, "Child, what **are** you talking about? I never said anything to Mardine about getting you over here."

Rosie realized it was another one of Mardine's tricks. But she was so happy it didn't matter. She grabbed Little John's hand and started swinging him around. She felt like she was floating on a cloud. Though she never expected to see Blake at this picnic, in the back of her mind she had been wishing he might be there. And who knew he could sing like that. WOW! And he still called her his wife!

So, a new thought would burden her mind now, "How do I get into Ballard?"

CHAPTER 6

LIVES TURNED UPSIDE DOWN

The main enemy of cotton farmers, the boll weevil, packed up millions of his family and said, "Let's see what Georgia is like." Cotton was not expected to be a good crop that year. Lance and Mabel packed up their family and moved north to Cleveland, Ohio. Daniel pushed his luck and planted a small cotton crop anyway. When it was time to pick, he actually had a decent crop.

Meanwhile, Rosie started working on her plan right after the spring picnic. From the time she was a young girl, she had had problems with her legs. She had days when her legs actually hurt so much, she could barely walk to the table to eat. Whether it was growing pains or arthritis, the doctor didn't know. She decided to use this ailment as part of her plan. By that year's cotton-picking time Mama and Papa both agreed to excuse her from picking.

"Why can't Rose pick cotton?"

"Something is wrong with her legs; you know that."

"She seems to do alright when she's chasing after those boys."

"Don't worry yourself about Rose, just do what YOU are supposed to do, Mardine."

When school started, she would come home crying about the long walk. She missed some school days telling her parents her legs hurt too bad to go. Daniel was adamant about his kids going to school. It was he who brought up the idea of Ballard School for his daughter. Rosie could not believe her plan was working.

Her parents scraped together the tuition fee of two dollars and forty cents per month to send Rosie to a school 30 miles away from home. Rosie was satisfied, Mardine was angry, and Daniel was pleased his daughter would receive a good education. Later Rosie would look back and see that her scheme worked to her detriment. The education Rosie received at Ballard Normal School began in the classroom and ended in the cemetery between the Ballard Congregational Church and the Girls Dormitory.

On her first day on campus, the counselor suggested her time would be well spent if she got involved in the school and extracurricular activities right away. "Jump in with both feet," the small, thin, pointed-nose young counselor laughingly instructed the young girl. Away from home and alone for the first time, Rosie forgot the reason why she was at Ballard Normal School and joined the volleyball team.

The first week she spent adjusting to the change in curriculum, trying to learn the rules, and learning her way around campus. She always kept her eye out for Blake and, maybe, spotted him a couple of times. She easily made friends with the girls in her dormitory, never mentioning Blake to them.

Two weeks after she arrived on campus, she saw Blake for the first time. On Tuesday, after leaving class on her way to volleyball practice, she saw him with a bunch of young men sitting on the steps of the main school. They appeared to be studying. She walked up behind him and in a voice only he could hear, she said, "Guess who goes to Ballard now?"

Blake immediately recognized the voice, jumped up, turned around, grabbed Rosie in a bear-hug and swung her around. In a very loud voice he said, "Gentlemen, gentlemen, attention please! I would like to introduce you to the woman I have chosen to be my wife."

Rosie's face flushed crimson. The group of unfamiliar faces stared at her waiting, as Blake continued to swing her around, for Rosie to deny or confirm his statement. Then quickly he whisked her down the path away from his amazed friends, yelling back, "See you guys."

The questions started. "Why are you here? When did you get here? What are you doing here? What's going on? Talk to me, Girl!" He wanted to kiss her but respected her enough not to do something like that in front of everyone.

Rosie was overwhelmed. She saw a girl from her dormitory walk by looking at Blake hugging her. "Let me catch my breath. You sure know how to surprise a girl even when she tries to surprise you."

The happy couple found an unoccupied bench and sat and talked until it was time for volleyball practice. They collaborated on their schedules so they could plan when to see each other. They were shocked that they had one class right next to each other. Blake held her hand and thanked her for working it so they could be together. "I knew when I first met you, we would be together."

Word got around campus quickly about Blake and Rosie and their close relationship. Rosie's roommates questioned her about her boyfriend, "Why didn't you tell someone that you are almost engaged to one of the most handsome boys on campus?"

"And, boy, can he sing!" one girl announced.

Although Rosie told everyone they were close friends, Blake was telling everyone they were almost married. Eventually, they were an item.

Blake's friends' conversations were coarser than those of the girls in Rosie's dorm. One guy, Jonadab, wanted to know the details of the relationship. Many times he asked Blake how close he and his lady were—trying to get to the details of their relationship without coming out and asking if they had had sex. He was shocked to find out that they had never even kissed. "Man, what's wrong with you?" Jonadab was filled with stories about different girls that he had. "That's why my parents sent me to this school. They're hoping a new kind of religion would cure me. I got a bug that I don't ever want to be cured. I'll tell you man, once you try it, you'll always want it. Man, I could see me and that woman of yours……whoooo! If you were man enough, Blake, you couldn't walk away without trying a little bit of that. Be careful somebody else don't please her before you do. Man, you know she wants it just as bad as you. Don't let her fool you."

Jonadab talked about sex all the time. He brought a bunch of explicit pictures with him to school. He showed the pictures to everyone who wanted to see them, even a couple of girls. "Yeah, those are the kind of girls I like to spend time with, if you know what I mean."

Blake found himself listening to Jonadab more and more, and he liked to look at those pictures.

Rosie and Blake found time and places to be alone on campus. Eventually their togetherness graduated beyond the handshake. Her friend Nola saw them kissing on the stairs when they thought no one was watching. Nola warned Rosie that she might be getting into something she couldn't handle. Rosie ignored her, maybe because she had fallen so hard for Blake, or maybe she was just too naïve.

Then the conversations started. Listening over and over to the stories Jonadab told, Blake weakened. He forgot about the respect that he had for Rosie. He forgot about the chance of pregnancy, he forgot about his own self-respect; he just wanted to have sex with Rosie. He tried to be polite and ask Rosie if she would have sex, but she always told him no. Eventually, he talked about sex all the time. He accused her of teasing him. When they were alone his hands started to touch and search.

Rosie fought him off more than once. Realizing that he had changed into a different person, Rosie took Nola's advice and stayed away from Blake. It hurt her not to spend time with him. She tried to spend more time with her female friends, but she missed him so much.

Blake missed her too. When Jonadab came into the room and saw Blake glumly lying on the bed, he told him he needed to go get his girl and have sex with her. "That's all you need. man. You want me to hook you up? One of the hoochies I know would **kill** to let you touch 'em up!"

Blake could not get his mind straight. He had to shake this feeling.

That night when Rosie came out of volleyball practice, Blake was waiting for her. "Hey Pretty Rosie, may I walk you back to the dorm?"

The other girls went on ahead and Blake and Rosie lingered along the path. Blake asked her to take the long way through the cemetery. Rosie loved hearing him call her "Pretty Rosie" again, yet everything in her was saying "NO!" She had always avoided that cemetery as if there were something evil in it. But because she had missed Blake so much and they had not talked for a while, she agreed to go that way. She just wanted to be with him. As they walked, Blake told her how much he missed her. His voice was low and hesitant. She could barely hear what he was saying; he seemed nervous. He told her she didn't understand what he'd been going through. Then he talked about how beautiful she was and how happy he was when he was with her. Then, suddenly he stopped talking and walking–as if he had reached a chosen spot.

The sun was setting beneath an orange glow on the horizon. Crickets were starting to chirp and birds were saying good-night to the day. The Ballard Normal School teenagers stopped by a grave where someone had placed fresh flowers. Rosie felt a chill come over her, but before she could react, Blake threw her down, tore off her underpants, and held her while he dropped his pants that he had already unzipped.

Then he raped her.

Rosie did not know how long she lay on top of the grave before she felt she could move.

Blake violated her, then jumped up and ran. He ran!

He left her bruised and lying there amidst the white flowers that had been placed on the grave in honor of "MOTHER." Now, she thought those flowers were for the bereavement of ROSIE MILLER. She wanted to be below the ground with "MOTHER." The choked and gulping sound she heard was her own sobbing. As evening began to darken, she was afraid to move and afraid not to. She jumped when she felt something crawling across her face. That crawly thing, whatever it was, made her pull herself up and get back to the dormitory before she could no longer find her way in the dark.

When she entered her room scratched, stained, and scarred–mentally and physically–no one was there. She was ashamed and hurting. She sobbed in the bathtub as long as she could, not knowing who to turn to or what to do. When the other girls arrived laughing and giggling about a boy who had smiled at Nola, she was in bed pretending to be asleep. She wanted to yell a warning at the top of her voice, "Run! Run and don't ever let them touch you. I can show you what they do."

Her mind was filled with hate for Blake. She would never forget the look in his eyes as he held her down while she was screaming for him to stop. It was the look of a mad man. In her mind she saw him as the devil himself. How could he do this to her? She thought she could kill him. If she reported him to the school administrators, she didn't care what they did to him. But what would they think of her? Everyone would think she was the kind of girl who had sex and messed around with boys. Did she entice Blake to do this as Nola had been telling her? Was this her fault?

Was this the consequence of her tricking Papa into sending her to Ballard? Over and over one word rolled through her aching, defiled body from head to toe....*hate, hate, hate, hate.*

The room was quiet except for the ticking clock. Her roommates were sleeping the steady breaths of innocence. They were unblemished; they had no reason to stay awake. *What will they think of me? Do they already know? Did they see me come back with blood on my clothes? Maybe it was really me they were laughing at.* The clock was ticking louder and louder as she wanted to yell and scream, but she lay there quietly, still and tormented. Tick Tock. Tick Tock.

Pregnant? She would be unable to live through the shame of becoming pregnant. She thought if she were pregnant, she would kill herself. If she were pregnant she knew she could not look at her father. She would be a disgrace to her family, and she knew he would surely kill her before she could kill herself. What could she say? They had scraped and saved money to pay for her to go to Ballard and now this. It was three weeks until her period; then, she would know.

By daylight she made up her mind she would not tell anyone what happened. She would wait three weeks to see if her period came and if it did not, she would kill herself. People could think whatever they wanted. At least she would save her family the embarrassment of having an unwed teenage pregnant daughter. She would force herself to get through these next three weeks, because this might be the last three weeks of her life. It startled her when Suzie, the human alarm clock, started sneezing, as she did every morning at seven o'clock.

Today was the last basketball practice. Her dilemma had snatched her mind, heart, energy and senses and had them rolling around in her body like sagebrush in a whirlwind.

Nola asked her, "What's wrong? You look sick. Do you want me to let your teachers know so you can go lie down?"

The lack of food and sleep gave her a zombie-like appearance, but she forced herself through classes the whole day. With one look at her, the basketball coach readily excused her from the game assuming her illness was legitimate.

The next day, Friday, Brent came to watch the last game and take Rosie home for the weekend. She stood outside the gym, almost around the corner, not wanting to answer her friends' questions of why she was not playing. As she watched the other students go by, she thought she saw Blake. She stepped back so he would not see her. She let out a sigh of relief when she saw Brent coming. Her relief faded when she saw two people in the wagon. This Friday for the first time ever, he brought Mardine.

As she stepped to the edge of the road her face was longer than her bag of laundry.

"You look like you're ready to go home. What about the game?"

"I'm not going to play today; I'm not feeling very good."

Mardine looked her up and down. "Yeah, you look like something the cat drug in and the kittens didn't want. I hope you didn't catch a plague or something down here at this ritzy school."

Mardine helped her sister with her bags and got in the back of the wagon so Rosie could sit up front with Brent. As Brent started up the horses Mardine said, "You think you feel bad now, wait until you get home."

Rosie's heart started to pound, and her head snatched around to look at Mardine. What did she know? How could she know? Did everybody know? She got hot and her eyes started to well up as Mardine, who was especially bubbly today continued to rant on.

"You want to know what I know?"

The tail on the horse was swishing back and forth and the buildings of Ballard were passing by really fast as they left the campus. Rosie was trying to hold back the tears while Mardine talked, "Home will never be the same. Papa is so angry I thought he was going to kill somebody. Everybody is walking around afraid to say anything." Rosie was sure Mardine was talking about her, and the tears started to flow.

"Mama tried to calm Papa down. He threw his hat across the room and almost knocked his dinner off the table. She told him he had to expect this was going to happen sooner or later. He didn't want to hear it. He won't talk to anybody. Mama asked him a question and he went out the door and slammed the screen. It almost came off the hinges."

"Mama told her not to worry, everything would work out."

Now Rosie was confused. Mama told *who* not to worry? What would work out? She was afraid to ask, but she had to know what Mardine knew.

She asked Mardine in a soft, hesitant voice, "What are you talking about?"

Mardine yelled, "Annie! Annie is getting married."

Rosie's anxiety eased. She felt better than she had for the last two days. At least the focus was on something other than her problem.

"When did this all happen? I've just been gone a week."

Then Mardine told her the story of Annie and her boyfriend Robert, words spewing out of her mouth. "Robert was going north and wanted to take Annie with him. So, he asked Papa, could they marry? And Papa said no. But Annie and Mama said yes. So Papa is mad as blazes; I mean, madder than blazes!"

When Rosie got home she had a long talk with Annie who had been in love with Robert for a long time. He had asked her to marry him last year, but she was afraid to ask Papa and kept putting him off. Papa wanted her to go to school and become a teacher. Annie wanted to get married and have children. She had to wait to see what Papa would let her do.

The weekend flew and soon Rosie was on her way back to Ballard. On the trip to town, she noticed that Brent was unusually quiet. Thinking back, she realized he had talked only a little when they were going home. "Brent, are you alright? Do you have something on your mind?" Rosie's voice was kind and she was sincere. They saw each other less and less, but he was still her favorite brother.

Brent hesitated. "Well, actually all this business with Annie has upset my plans, Rosie. I've finally decided to tell Papa that I'm going north to work on my art. Now, I'm afraid it's the wrong time. I don't want to bring it up."

Now he knew he had to wait.

It was the third weekend and Rosie had not had her period. She knew she was pregnant. She realized everyone would eventually know, and fear made her become irrational. There was only one week left of school. She could not face her family with such grim news, so she planned what she was going to do when Brent took her home on Friday.

After dinner was over and the kitchen cleaned, after all her clothes were washed, she slipped out in the bushes and picked a handful of poison berries. She hid them in a jar in her bedroom. That night after everyone was asleep, she opened the lid. Hours went by while she sat there looking at the berries in the moonlight streaming through the window. She tried to put her hand in the jar and take out the berries, but she could not do it. Her pajamas were wet with perspiration and tears.

I have to do it. I have to do it. I can't face Papa. I have to do it, she said to herself, but she could not. Before daylight she took the jar outside and threw the berries away. She planned to accidentally break the jar the next day so no one would use the bottle and sicken or die.

Next morning when she went into the yard to break the jar, she saw the basket of old tools. Deep in the basket was an old straight razor that was too rusty for shaving. She took it and hid in her book. *Maybe I can't kill myself, but I surely can kill Blake*, she decided.

She had only seen Blake once since the incident. On Monday she looked until she saw him coming down the hall. Her life had changed drastically; his life was about to end. Everything was working out as she had planned. She put down her head until they were nearly face to face. He looked at her, and she looked up with a fake smile as if she wanted to talk to him.

He came closer, not knowing what he could say. He had his head down as usual, not making eye contact. Rosie had her hand in her book on the open razor. When Blake got within striking distance, she dragged the razor across his chest. He jumped back before the razor went too deep, but blood began to spurt out over their books and the floor. Students screamed and ran.

Rosie was sitting in the principal's office with her blouse covered with blood. The principal Mr. Pelokny asked Rosie why she had cut Blake, but she refused to talk. "I'm going to check on Blake and give you a few minutes to think, young lady," he told her.

He left the room to check on Blake. When he came back Rosie still would not talk to him.

In a loud, harsh voice, Mr. Pelokny said, "If you don't answer me, young lady, you will be expelled and will not graduate."

Mr. Pelokny left the room. When he returned, he told Rosie he was taking her home.

She never said a word. The teacher took Blake home and Mr. Pelokny took Rosie home.

Mama came out to meet the wagon wondering who was coming down the road that early in the day on a Monday afternoon. She screamed when she saw her daughter step down from the wagon with her blouse covered in blood. Papa was in the kitchen eating lunch and ran out when he heard Mama scream.

Mr. Pelokny told Mr. and Mrs. Daniel Miller what their daughter had done. Although they were relieved that the blood was not Rosie's, they could not believe that Rosie had done what Mr. Pelokny said. They tried to talk with her while Mr. Pelokny was there, but she held her head down and said nothing. Not a tear fell from her eyes. Papa shook his head at her stubbornness.

Rosie and Mama sat silently in the room as Papa walked Mr. Pelokny to his wagon. Papa told Mr. Pelokny that he would get to the bottom of this and talk to him later. Papa stood there for about five minutes and watched the wagon go down the road. Before he came in, he took a walk around the house.

When Papa trudged into the room, his face was sad and drawn. He sat down beside Rosie. His voice was low and soft. "Rosie, I don't know why you did what you did, but I know you're not the type of person to try to cut someone unless they did something awful to you." Then he did something she only remembered him doing once before: he put his arms around her and hugged her tight.

"Rosie, maybe I haven't said this to you enough, but I love you. I want you to know that whatever happened, you can tell me and your Mama."

Wrapped in Papa's arms, Rosie let open the floodgates. She cried long and hard. When she could talk, she told him everything. She told him that Blake had become too frisky and she stopped talking to him. And she sobbed about that night when he said he would walk her home. She couldn't tell him what Blake did, but she told him how he left her there when he was finished, "He left me lying there in the cemetery. He ran. He ran away."

Then she told him she was pregnant.

When the word "pregnant" came out of her mouth, she was afraid to look at Papa. She told him that she had tried to kill herself by eating the poison berries but did not have the nerve to do it. Papa hugged her again. She watched the tears rolling down his face; that only made her cry more.

"I couldn't kill myself, so I wanted to kill him."

Rosie cried and sobbed for about twenty minutes.

Papa said, "Mama, Rosie, change your clothes and wash your face. We gotta take a ride."

It was a half hour ride to the Maxwell house. Rosie sat in the back of the wagon dreading facing anyone else. She had only seen Blake's parents twice before. She wished she had the straight razor that Mr. Pelokny took from her. If Blake denied what he had done, she was going to finish the job.

Mr. Maxwell came out and asked them to come in. Blake was standing there with blood still on his clothes. The teacher at school had taped his wound to stop the bleeding. He was obviously scared. Looking down as usual, his chin was digging a hole in his chest.

Mr. Maxwell, a tall dark-skinned man who looked exactly like an older version of Blake, was snorting and pacing like a wild bull. He told Papa he was ashamed and disappointed in his son. Then he looked at Blake and asked him what he had to say for himself.

The tears rolled down onto the bloody shirt. Blake was trembling all over. Through his sobs he tried to talk. "It was the pictures and the talk." Sob… sob… "They talked about women all the time" …sob..sob… "They told me she wanted me to do it." ….sob. sob.. "My friends told me I had to do it to be a man." ..sob.. sob.. "But as soon as I did I knew I had done something so terrible I was damned. Then I knew I would be a man if I didn't do it." Sob…sob…. "I knew saying I'm sorry was not enough. I love Rosie." …sob ..sob….. "I want to marry her."

Until now Rosie had said not a word. Anger sent the words and tears spilling. She glared at him with all the hate and venom she could muster. With her eyes narrowed, Rosie looked at Blake who had stopped sobbing and was watching her. Her voice was quiet but sharp, "Marry you? Marry you? I don't even want to look at you," she spit at him. "When I leave here today, I never want to lay eyes on you again in my life, ever again." She turned and went to the wagon to wait for her parents.

Daniel was so angry he could barely finish his sentence, "Mr. and Mrs. Maxwell, my daughter is pregnant. She will not graduate from school because of what your son did to her. There is no excuse. Your son has messed up our daughter's life."

He turned to Blake, "You will have a responsibility for this baby even if she does not want to see you," he jerked his head in Rosie's direction. "You and I; we WILL talk later. But right now, I've had about as much of you as I can take," Daniel looked at Blake with hatred and disgust as he followed his daughter.

When Brent heard what happened he took it upon himself to visit Blake. He met him in the fields and took revenge for his sister. Putting up no defense, Blake took the beating he felt he deserved. He was unable to go to his graduation because of some broken bones, which he claimed he didn't know how he got. After he healed his parents sent him to Detroit to live with his sister.

Mardine took the opportunity to rub Rosie's nose in the situation, "See, they sent you off to school, and then you go messing around until you get pregnant. Now I guess you're gonna have a little yella baby that I have to look at."

When Papa heard her, he told her never to say another thing about Rosie or they would have an appointment behind the shed. And that was the end of that.

Rosie was miserable. The first two months she went to church with her family because she thought no one knew. One Sunday one of the members told her she looked awful thick. "If I didn't know better, I'd swear you were pregnant."

After that Rosie refused to go to church.

CHAPTER 7

LITTLE GEORGE

Word gets around fast in a small town. People put two and two together: Blake left town after someone beat him to a pulp and Rosie was pregnant. Without knowing the whole story, her friends' parents prohibited them from having anything to do with her. She was ashamed of her condition, so she stayed on the Miller acreage for the whole summer. She could not take the stares and whispers she was sure to receive in town or at church.

It was a different kind of summer that year. Papa didn't plant very much cotton because the boll weevil was rampant in Georgia. Annie and Robert married and moved to Cleveland. Mardine went with them for the summer. John, Ed, and Rich did their chores and played baseball with the Miller family down the road. Rosie felt she would be pregnant forever as the hot, steamy days eased lazily along. The family did what they could to help her through her pregnancy. Mama kept her busy with work around the house. Papa sat and talked to her in the evening after dinner. Brent gave her rides in the wagon around the property, but time creeped by.

Rosie was mad at herself, mad at the world and hated Blake. She hated the baby. When she felt the baby move, she would curse him and Blake. She had thoughts about giving the baby away. She knew she did not want to look at it. If only this ordeal was over and she could go away and live a normal life.

When her time came, she had an easy delivery. Mama sent John to get Mother Wells when Rosie began her labor pains. After the baby pushed his way out she heard someone say, "What a fine baby boy!" They held him up

48

so she could see him, but she closed her eyes. She told Mother Wells she did not want to see or touch the baby. She lay there relieved that the delivery was over—not wanting to talk or move—just glad it was all over. They took the baby in the other room, and she heard him cry.

Brent came into the room and sat down beside her, rubbing her head with a wet cloth. "You OK, Rosie?" asked her kind brother. She nodded her head.

"Rosie, you have to take care of this baby," Brent held her hands as he spoke. "He needs your milk. He needs his mother. He is your flesh and blood no matter how he was conceived. I saw him and he is about as pretty as a boy can be. Please Rosie, just take a look at him. I'll help you. If you will be a mother to him, I will be a father and an uncle if you want me to."

Brent left the room and came back with the baby all cleaned up and smelling good. He laid him on Rosie's chest, and she looked down when she heard him whimper. When her eyes landed on that pretty, little, black. curly-headed boy, she fell in love. Her heart warmed to him. She brought him to her face and kissed him.

Brent's loud laugh brought Mama and Mother Wells back into the room. Mama felt the burden lifted as she saw her daughter accept her child.

"What you going to name him, Rosie?," Brent asked her quietly.

"Well, Brent, since you've offered to be a surrogate dad and uncle, I think it would be proper to name him after you. His name will be George."

After the baby was born, Rosie still refused to leave the Miller farm. She had fallen madly in love with the baby and doted on him all the time. Mardine was upset because she had to do her work and Rosie's, "All she does is sit around holding that crying baby."

When she visited Annie and Robert in Cleveland that summer, Mardine had told Aunt Mabel the whole story. Mabel had felt she was somewhat to blame because the two kids had formed a relationship while Rosie was helping her after she broke her leg those years ago. Mabel and Brent were really fond of each other. She knew her nephew was not the type of person who would rape a woman. She wrote to him and asked him to write her back and tell his side of the story.

He did:

Dear Aunt Mabel,

I was overjoyed to get your letter. I know the family is ashamed of me as they well should be.

At this point Mabel thought he was admitting to everything.

First, I want to tell you that I love Rosie. I was smitten the first time I saw her. I know you must ask, "How could you have done what you did, if you love her?" What I did was, without a doubt, morally wrong, wicked, and sinful. I have no excuses. There was so much going on in my head, it was like I was possessed. It all started when I became fascinated with some pictures I should not have been looking at. My roommates gave me many pictures with sexual content and their conversation was always about sex and how good it was. I feel embarrassed talking to you about this, but I want you to know what led up to my bad decisions.

Rosie stopped talking to me when I tried to encourage her to do wrong. We had become very close, but she was not willing to go to the next level. I knew she liked me; I was so mixed up. My roommates told me she was teasing me, and she wanted to have sex as bad as I did. They told me they saw her flirting with someone and if I didn't do it, she would do it with someone else. They told me I was not a man until I did. I never thought I would force her. That day I waited for her after practice. I missed her; I wanted to be near her. I thought I could walk and talk with her. We walked through the cemetery, and I could smell the aroma of one I wanted to touch among all the dead in that place. When I saw the white flowers on the grave something took control of me. It was like I was looking at our wedding flowers. In my mind's eye I saw Rosie walking down the aisle to me in a white dress. I don't even remember pulling off her clothes. When I came to my senses, I heard her screaming and the devil himself was standing above me laughing. I was so afraid I jumped up and ran. I could not believe what I did.

After it happened, I was not man enough to go to her and apologize. I avoided her at school. I never even thought about her getting pregnant until her father and mother brought her to our home. When I met Brent on the road, I knew he was going to beat me up. I would have done the same for my sister's honor. I graduated, but she didn't, because of me. I heard that she had our baby boy. I wish I could see him, if only I could make up for all the wrong I've done. If only I could make her believe that I love her and that I regret my behavior. I am full of sorrow, regrets, and suffering. The crazy thing is I understand how she feels, and I do not expect her to ever forgive me, but I wish she would. I pray that God will have mercy on me. I hope you will understand and forgive me too.

Thank you for writing.
Love, Blake

Mabel hoped there would be something in his letter to vindicate him, but there wasn't. Still she felt compassion and wanted to help. Mabel's plot was to get Rosie out of Macon and up to Cleveland. Then, she would work on getting Blake to communicate with her. Maybe if she, herself, talked enough to Rosie she could get her to see how remorseful Blake was.

Rosie was lethargic as she sat on the back porch holding George and watching Brent take Mardine to a school party. Mardine looked pretty in the dress trimmed in lace that Annie had given her when she spent the summer in Cleveland. Rosie did Mardine's hair, a skill she had learned during her tenure at Ballard. Her heart hurt knowing that she was missing all the parties she should be going to. Then she looked down at George's smiling face. He reached up his arms to her. He was so beautiful. She loved him more than her lost youth, more than parties, more than anything.

"This is not what I planned my life to be, but thank you, God, for this blessing."

She heard the horn blow signaling the arrival of the mailman. She carried George down the path to the mailbox. The letter from Mabel was a pleasant surprise. This was an option she never had considered. If she could get out of Macon maybe she could start a life with her baby. Mabel said she it would be better to raise a son in the north than that lynching south. She told her that she had talked with Annie, and Annie wanted to help her too. Mabel said she would even send her train fare.

Rosie ran to find Mama to share this news with her.

CHAPTER 8

ROSIE MOVES NORTH

It was February after all the letters went back and forth and arrangements were finally made for Rosie and George to go north. She apologized to Brent for leaving Macon before him as he took her to the station. When he helped her on the train, he kissed her and George goodbye. He kissed George again and grabbed Rosie's arm. "Wait Rosie, I think your baby has a fever." She felt his head, and before she could say anything he threw up all over her. Brent put them back on the wagon and took them home.

A long month later they successfully made the trip to Cleveland.

Mabel waited until Rosie was comfortable in her surroundings before she set her scheme in motion. She wrote Blake and told him Rosie had moved in with her. He immediately wrote back and sent money for Rosie and the baby with a personal note for Rosie. Mabel did not show Rosie until she received the second letter from him. When Rosie demanded to know how he knew she was there, Mabel said that she had told him. Still, Rosie would not respond to him.

Two months after Rosie was there, Blake came to Cleveland. It was the first time she had seen him since her parents took her to his parent's house. Rosie would not talk to him and avoided him as much as possible while he was there. He was happy to see the baby and spent a lot of time playing with him.

Each month when Blake came to Mabel and Lance's house to see Rosie and the baby, he brought gifts and money. Even though Rosie could hardly stand to look at Blake, she started to acknowledge him on his third visit. On the fifth visit they had a conversation.

She talked, but she was cold and distant. Before he raped her, she had loved him. She often thought of him saying that one day he would marry her. But from the moment he raped her–and left her– she hated everything about him.

Mabel asked Rosie to read the letter Blake had written to her describing his remorse. She read it, dropped it on the table, and did not comment. Rosie knew that Blake was sending money to pay for her and George's upkeep. She wanted to get a job, but it was hard for her to leave the house. She spent most of her time cleaning, cooking, and picking up after Lance, Mabel, and their children. She earned a couple of dollars doing hair for Mabel and her friends. Mabel kept her busy because she did not want Rosie to get a job and discover she could make it on her own without Blake.

On the weekend that Blake came to visit her, Rosie would busy herself scrubbing floors or washing walls. She let Blake and George spend time together. George looked forward to seeing his daddy. Rosie was busy on her hands and knees scrubbing the bathroom floor. Blake knocked on the open door, "Rosie, would you take a break and come talk to me out on the porch?"

"No, I'm busy. Whatever it is you have to say, you can just say it right there." She kept scrubbing, paying close attention to one little spot on the floor that would not go away.

Blake tried again, "Rosie, would you stop scrubbing long enough to hear what I have to say? I want you to be sure to hear everything I have to say." They went to the front room and sat down. Mabel and Lance took little George and went into the kitchen and put their ears to the wall to listen.

"Rosie, please hear me out before you respond." He was looking Rosie in the eye instead of looking down as was his custom. "There are some things you should know. I know you still hate me and maybe you always will. I've never asked you to forgive me, because I feel you are justified to feel as you do."

Blake had to stop and take deep breaths. *I must give it a try*, he steeled himself. (Deep breath.)

"Please forgive me. Please know that I made the worst mistake of my life. There is something else you need to know," he hesitated, took a deep breath, and said, "I love you more than life itself. I love you and our son

54

with all my heart and soul. I pray all day long that you will see it in your heart to let me be a part of your life." (Deep breath.) Blake was crying and talking and breathing deep and hard. He kept eye contact until he said everything he had to say.

"I want to ask you to marry me." (Deep breath) "I will take good care of you and George. He needs a father, and I will be the best dad in the world to him and the best husband to you. You both need me. I have two jobs and an apartment in Detroit. Please let me try to make up for the wrong I have done."

Rosie was not crying. She had a hard, contemptuous look on her face. She felt her temperature rise with all the shame and hate she had stored up during the last two years. It didn't make sense to marry the man who raped you. The offer did not appeal to her until he said George's name. She knew she could probably provide for herself and her George, but she wanted the best for her child. For him, she was willing to sacrifice her pride.

Rosie spoke her mind evenly, "The first day I saw you I was smitten by the words as sweet as honey pouring from your mouth. Your words were sweet; I wonder if your heart was evil then. I fell for all those lines you gave me about marrying me. Now, I feel that was just to build my trust so you could take advantage of me. You say you felt that you were possessed when you raped me. How do I know you won't become possessed again? How do I know you are not possessed now?"

He understood her suspicions. Looking her in the eye Blake said, "Rosie, I have acted like a demon, but since then I have returned to the faith that I knew from a child. I have reconnected with the Lord, and I know he has forgiven me. I was listening and trusting the wrong people, but now I am trusting in God. I have turned my life around knowing what it takes to be a man, a husband, and a father. I pray to God that you will give me the opportunity to show you how I have changed."

She looked up in Blake's face. Her voice was strong and her words were direct. When she opened her mouth she heard herself go against everything she had repeated to herself since that day at the cemetery, "I believe what you say is true. Yes, George needs a father, but after what you did to me, I can't think of having any man in my life, least of all you. I hate you with every ounce of my being. I took all the stares, whispers, gossip, and name-calling because of you. I wore the banner of shame. I couldn't graduate. I lost my friends, my family was disgraced, and the money they spent to send me to school was wasted. That is what I dwelled on daily while I built a castle of hate for you."

"I hated the baby growing in my body because of the devil that put his seed in me. The day he was born I didn't want to look at him. When I saw him, he had your mark. He looked just like you. God works in mysterious ways, and he melted my heart through that helpless little creature who reached out for me."

"I'm going to surprise you with my answer. In fact, I'm surprising myself. For this child I will marry you, move to Detroit, and live as your wife, but I will not **be** your wife. What I'm doing, I do for him. I'm determined that my child will have a good life. When I first met you, I was a young girl looking for attention. Now, I'm a mother looking for attention to my son. I came to Cleveland for his benefit and I will go to Detroit for his benefit."

"What's done is done," Rosie said with finality. "You can't unscramble an egg. But know this: If you ever lay a hand on me again; if you ever touch me again, I'll find someone to take care of George and I'll finish the job that I started on you at Ballard School. I'm as sure of that as I'm sure I deeply love my child. If you want to withdraw the invitation, I understand."

Blake did not hesitate. "I am sure this is what I want. I want you and George with me."

Rosie heard Mabel, who was listening from the kitchen, yell, "Praise the Lord-na."

One month later at the home of Lance and Mabel, with her sister Annie as her bridesmaid, Rosie became Mrs. Blake Maxwell. Blake took his family home to Detroit.

CHAPTER 9

A HOME IN DETROIT

In less than a week Rosie had transformed the small drab kitchenette into a cheerful home. New curtains, flowers, and the smell of food cooking works wonders for a bachelor's apartment. She washed the windows, scrubbed the floors, and decorated the walls with pictures that she bought at the dime store.

When Blake came home from his work at the furniture store, he welcomed the smell of a full-course meal waiting for him. After a delicious dinner he would spend time with George until bedtime, after which he would go down to the barber shop and shine shoes. When he returned, he would find Rosie sleeping in George's room.

The apartment looked homey–warm and cozy–but the coldness between Blake and Rosie made it an ice house. She only talked to him when she had to, and usually that was about George. She never came near enough to touch him. She left her smile in Macon. She was stressed and depressed and didn't know how to shake out of it. She wanted to laugh, sing, and talk. But she didn't know how to lose her anger.

On Sundays, Blake took George to church with him. He always asked Rosie to join them, but she refused. After they left, she would cry until their return. She asked God, often, if there were any hope for a better life, if not for her own sake, at least, for George. She knew she was unpleasant to be around.

Then one Sunday, when Blake asked her to join them for church, she surprised them both and said "Yes!"

The congregation welcomed her when the Maxwells came in. Everyone knew George. They complimented Rosie on her son and shared many stories about him from previous Sundays. Though she felt conspicuous, she was determined to make it through this day. *It's time to grow, Rose*, she told herself. Blake found a seat for his family and then left them to sing in the choir. That Sunday he performed a solo. The song was "LOVE." Each time he said the word "love" he looked directly into Rosie's eyes.

> "Though I speak as men and angels do -
> Without love I am noise to you.
> I moved mountains, I had the gift of prophecy.
> I had knowledge and understood all mystery.
> To the poor I gave all-even my body to flames.
> I sacrificed all, nothing did I gain.
> Love is patient and kind, keeps no record of wrong-
> No envy, not selfish, it suffers long.
> I have faith, I have hope, sent from above.
> But the greatest of all is Love, Love, Love.
> Love will not behave indecently.
> Nor will it rejoice in iniquity.
> Childish things love does not embrace.
> Love sees through the mirror face to face.
> Love, believes, endures, hopes all things.
> Yes I believe in love that is why I sing…
> Though imperfect things may pass away…
> .Perfect love will always stay.
> I have faith, I have hope, sent from above.
> But the greatest of all is Love, Love, Love…"

Blake ended the song holding the word "LOVE" for a long time. He kept his eyes on Rosie though the song had ended and the last note had died. As the room became warm, her frozen heart began to melt. Blake saw it as he continued to stare at her. He did not hear the young girls swooning or the congregation applauding. He didn't hear the "Amens," but he saw the love in her eyes.

He saw what he had been looking for ever since he went to Aunt Mabel's house to see Rosie in Cleveland. He had looked for it when he asked her to marry him and move to Detroit. He had searched her eyes when she repeated the wedding vows. Every morning when he went to work and every evening when he came home, he hoped that he would see it. Just a spark. Just a tiny spark that could start a fire. And there it was. He saw love in her eyes.

That day the ice house started to thaw…a smile.. drip, drip, drip. A month went by … a few words…. drip, drip, drip. Two months…a touch…drip, drip, drip…and three months later, the ice was gone. Rosie became his wife. They laughed, they talked, and they sang. They planned, they went on walks, and they consummated their marriage. The first time, when Blake had forced her, he had sex. This time they made love. He took his time and was gentle. There was joy in the Maxwell house. There was not a happier man in Detroit than Blake Maxwell. Even little George knew their ice house had warmed up.

Blake could not stop singing the Christmas carols of peace and love. His rich voice bounced around the apartment:

> "Joy to the world, the Lord is come!
> Let earth receive her King.
> Let every heart prepare Him room
> And heaven and nature sing
> And heaven and nature sing
> And heaven, and heaven and nature sing!"

For him, heaven and nature did sing–every day. His love practically resounded for Rosie and the grace she had granted him and their family. He sang,

> "He rules the world with truth and grace
> And makes the nations prove (and makes the nations prove)
> And glories of His righteousness
> And wonders of His love
> And wonders of His love
> And wonders of His love
> And wonders, wonders of His love
> And wonders, wonders of His love."

This would be the first real Christmas for his family. He went to work happy and came home happy. Not as many shoes got shined at the barber shop now, because Blake spent more time at home. The barbers teased him about being in such a good mood. "We know what's going on at your house Blake Maxwell. All that love you're singing about ain't coming from the Lord."

Blake and Rosie worked together to save their money. And even though his boss, Mr. Perrin, gave Blake a sizable bonus, they spent sensibly on gifts at Christmas. They joined with their apartment neighbors and had a large Christmas potluck dinner. Rosie roasted a turkey and everyone brought a dish. They sang and danced. Fred from apartment 3-C rented a Santa costume and brought toys to the children. That night Blake and Rosie laid in bed and reminisced about the day. They were shocked to see dawn had met their happiness. Rosie told Blake that she was so happy and blessed that she had decided to join the church. Sunday, after church she would talk with the pastor.

Blake hugged, kissed her, and held her tight; he could not let her go. "This is the life I dreamed of when we used to sit on Aunt Mabel's porch. Thank you, God. Rosie, you are the only girl I have ever wanted. The only girl I have ever loved. The only girl I ever wanted to be with. I apologize for what I did." She told him she accepted his apology. When they heard George stirring, they tried to get a little rest before rising, but their love for each other robbed them of sleep.

When Blake came home from work on Friday night, he was sick. He told Rosie he could hardly breathe. She had noticed that Blake looked a little frail and had developed a consistent hard cough. He dismissed the suggestion that it might be from cigarettes. By Saturday morning, he was weaker. He refused to go to the doctor, not wanting to spend their savings. That Sunday they stayed home so Blake could rest.

Even though he was getting weaker he insisted on going to work. By midweek Mr. Perrin took him to the doctor. After a battery of tests, it was revealed that Blake had tuberculosis. The recommended treatment for tuberculosis was rest, good food, and fresh air. Tuberculosis was an airborne disease, highly contagious. Blake could not stay in the house with his family. He was admitted to a sanitarium.

For the first six months, Blake could have no visitors, but that didn't stop the lovebirds from writing every day. Rosie cried reading the letter from Blake to six-year-old George, telling him he was now the man of the house and had to take good care of his mother. After his mother read the letter, he went into his bedroom. When she went in to console him, she found him on his knees praying. Later, he told his mother that he had to take care of her and pray every day like his daddy did.

After six months Rosie and George were excited to take the long ride to the sanitarium. George cried when his daddy could not come home. Once a month they went back to visit. After six months Rosie realized he was not improving, he looked weaker than he did when he left home. His cough was harsher, and when he started coughing, he could not stop. For the first time she was afraid Blake was dying.

Rosie called his sister and asked her to notify the family that Blake was not improving. Her hope of his recovery waned. She had been so sure the hospital would heal him, and that he would be home soon. He continued to deteriorate. By the time his sister came to see him, he was barely alive. Maybe it was the cigarettes. Maybe it was because he would not go to the doctor until his condition was too far gone. Maybe it was because he was a black male, or maybe it was his time. Whatever the reason, with his wife at his side, Blake succumbed.

George, the man of the house, was seven years old when his father died.

Mr. Perrin had been Blake's boss and also his friend. When Blake started working at the small furniture store, Mr. Perrin noticed he was very quiet and kept to himself. Time passed and they spent time working closely together. Eventually during their conversations, Blake told him his life story and how he had turned his life over to God. Mr. Perrin felt compassion for Blake, and they became friends. Mr. Perrin told many people, including his own relatives, that Blake was the best worker he ever had. His passing was as if a close family member had died. He wanted to be involved in the funeral, so he asked Rosie if he could pay for it.

The sun shone outside as they sat in the dismal church looking at the emaciated body lying in the open casket. The small church that Blake was loyal to was bursting at the seams that day. Many who knew and loved him filled the pews. The people from the Christmas party felt like they had lost their brother. The barbers from the barber shop remembered how happy he had become right before he got sick. The men who would never have shoes shined the way Blake shined them came in with dusty shoes in his honor. Women who had swooned when Blake sang hymns, boo-hooed louder than Rosie, George, and Blake's sisters. The minister cried during the sermon. Mr. Perrin was so upset his wife had to help him leave the church before the service was over. There was a cloud over everyone's heart.

Rosie held her head down as she tried to keep her composure for George, but he felt her body tremble as she quietly and continually sobbed. After all they had been through, the love they finally had for each other, and now this. Her body felt hollow. She felt like somebody, or something, had reached inside of her when they pronounced Blake dead, and yanked the marrow from her bones and the breath from her body. She was amazed she could breathe because she felt there was no breath left in her. When George asked if Daddy was sleeping the church began to close in around Rosie.

Before the funeral was over, Rosie stood up, composed herself and turned to the congregation in the church, "God bless you all, I thank you for coming. I want to say something before all of you. I loved Blake. We had some bad times, but I learned to love him. I love him, I love him. I don't know what is before me and George, but we have something that we can keep in our hearts for the rest of our lives. We know he loved us with all his heart. Thank you, Blake, I will always love you."

After the funeral the family went to Rosie's place and had a roundtable discussion about Rosie's future. Mardine, Annie, Brent, and Mama felt it was their appointed duty to make decisions for Rosie and George.

Mama suggested she move to Cleveland, "You must be used to the cold and snow already. It's just as bad in Cleveland."

Annie spoke up, "You know, since we moved to Cleveland, we're renting that nice house on Quincy. We have room until you find someplace of your own. You and the boy can't stay up here in Detroit by yourself. You'd have to get a job, and who's going to look after him while you work?"

Rosie did not respond.

Her friend Callie was in the kitchen helping out. When Rosie went to get her mother some water, Callie pulled her to the side and said quietly,

"Girl, ain't no way I'd go back and be up under my Mama no more. And that one sister didn't look happy at all when your Mama said you could stay with her. Don't you want to be on your own? You could go to school and get your license to do hair. You already know how; you just need your license. You better think about that. You can make a lot of money doing hair, enough to take care of you and your son."

While she was in the kitchen thinking about what Callie said and what Mama said, Rosie heard Mardine talking to Brent in the hallway. She was going on about the mess Rosie had made of her life and how she wants the family to take care of her.

In a low voice Rosie whispered to herself, "Thank you, Mardine, you just helped me make up my mind."

Mama was disappointed with Rosie's decision. She didn't want to leave Rosie in Detroit; Mardine didn't want Rosie to come to Cleveland; and Rosie didn't want to upset Mama. She sat there for a moment not saying anything. When Mama asked her to think it over before she made a final decision, Rosie told her then that she was sure she was going to stay.

"Well, Girl, if you've made up your mind, I guess that's it." Mama hesitated for a moment and then asked Rosie, "Would you consider one thing; can John stay with you? I would feel much better if I knew someone was here with you." Rosie liked that idea and agreed to it.

Grieving is personal. Everyone grieves in their own time. Rosie was so busy trying to adjust to her new life as the head of the household she didn't have time to grieve. She enrolled John in school, talked Mr. Perrin into giving her a part-time job, and enrolled herself in the Franklin School of Hair. The family had some semblance of a routine. Grieving had to wait.

The hospital told her as long as she paid something each month on Blake's hospital bill, they would not charge her interest. The proceeds from the life insurance policy that Blake had adamantly paid every week would cover her beauty school cost. The money she made from her part-time job with Mr. Perrin was enough for rent and utilities. The money Mama sent for John's upkeep was enough for food for the three of them.

She had assistance from various people. John was a big help. He cooked breakfast and was good with George. Mr. Perrin allowed her to study at work. Callie and the other neighbors helped out by fixing dinners or taking George and John away so she could get in the books. Winter and summer passed by quickly while she worked, went to school, studied, and took care of her family. It was far from easy, but she did it. She went to school six hours a day, studied four hours, worked four hours, and took care of her house, son, and brother. She did this for eighteen months. The hair-doing was not too hard, but the book-learning was difficult. There was so much to remember. She had to learn about bones, circulation, and vessels, almost like becoming a nurse.

And then it was over; she graduated. Time for life to begin.

CHAPTER 10

BESSIE'S SALON

She arrived fifteen minutes earlier than Bessie, the shop owner, had told her to be there. It started to rain on her pristine white uniform and white shoes. She visualized herself curling the nice lady's hair and the nice lady "ooohing and aahing" over her good work, giving her big money and big tips.

Bessie did not get there until thirty minutes after she said she would be there. The other hairdressers drifted in later. Bessie had told Rosie to come early so she could meet everyone before it got busy. But as soon as she opened the door, the customers ran in behind them. Bessie's introduction to everyone was lost in the mayhem. Rosie didn't know the difference between the operators and the customers.

One lady was standing in the front of the shop yelling for Cora. "She know I gotta go to work, don't tell me she's late again. I don't know why the hell I keep comin' in here, I know I can find somebody to do my hair when the say they gonna do it. Where the hell is that woman?"

Rosie was standing in the middle of the shop, and everyone was walking around her. She didn't know what she was supposed to do and where she was going to do it.

Cora ambled in and grabbed her customer and took her to the one shampoo bowl. As she approached Rosie standing there she asked who she was.

Before Rosie could answer Bessie yelled from the back, "That's Rosie, she's our new girl."

Cora reared back and looked at Rosie like she was looking at the landlord there to pick up past due rent. "Humph, you finally got a high yellow, half-white, stringy-haired, don't-know-nothing-but-to-stand around-in-the middle-of-the-floor girl. Wow, ain't that a hoot! How she gonna do some nappy hair when she got that stringy white hair? You is too much, Bessie. She pushed Rosie to the side with her customer and started the shampoo.

Bessie yelled to Cora that Minnie would shampoo for her until she got some customers. Cora yelled back that she was fine with that and made a fast turn to the front of the store and sat down and lit a cigarette.

Rosie didn't know where anything was. She was about to go to the back and ask Bessie to come and show her where they kept the shampoo when the customer started yelling for Cora to get her ass back there and wash her hair so she could go to work. "I don't want no nobody messing with my hair, come on Cora."

Cora yelled back, "Nah, she think she know everything, let her do it."

And that's how her day began. It just got worse after that. The salon was like a jungle: hot, smoky, loud, full of demanding, jealous, backstabbing co-workers and customers. All the time, it was hurry, hurry, hurry. Rosie soon learned that Bessie stayed in the back figuring her numbers all morning before she was ready to do hair. Laverne showed her where the shampoo was so she could wash Cora's customer's hair. When Rosie finished, the customer never said "Thank you," she just got up and went to Cora's station.

Cora yelled back, "Damn, they don't teach y'all how to wash hair no more in beauty school." She gave Rosie a mean look as she brought the customer back to the shampoo bowl and rinsed it again. The customer was mumbling that she just wanted to get her hair done and go to work.

The first three days all she did was shampoo for the experienced hairdressers. When they got behind, they asked her to curl. Then, customers started asking for her instead of their regular hairdressers. That didn't go over too well. Soon she had people standing in line for her to do their hair. The salon did not pay her as much as the experienced stylists, so she had to work harder and faster to make a decent living. She would drag home, half-dead trying to please a bunch of ungrateful, complaining women. The work was hard on her. She made one friend, Laverne. The rest of the ladies were jealous of her skill and did all they could to sabotage her. She kept to herself and didn't get into their gossip about whoever was not there. Cora called her stuck-up. Rosie never got over being called "high yellow, stringy-haired, no-nothing girl," the first day she got there.

Six months passed and Rosie was working twelve hours a day, six days a week. She was a fast learner and the best waver in the shop. Even though the others did not want to show her new and different techniques, she would watch, learn, and develop on her own. The women lined up for that special "Rosie wave" that would last longer than the other stylists.' Laverne told her to quit curling the hair so tight, "You want to make money don't you?" But Rosie did hair like she would want someone to do hers.

One Saturday, between the heat in the shop, and the tedious work schedule, she felt faint. She sat down and rested for a half-hour. Cora and the customers complained so she got up and continued waving. Once again, she felt dizzy, and this time, she passed out. When she came to, she was trembling all over. Bessie, the only one who had a car, took her to the hospital. She looked around at the white sterile hospital and it reminded her of the times she visited Blake. The trembling got worse. She thought she was dying.

After the examination the doctor sat her down and talked to her calmly. He held her hand and asked her why she was working so hard. "You are having a nervous breakdown." He told her to take off work for a month and whenever she went back, she was not to work as hard as she had been. "Are you trying to kill yourself?" he asked. "Because if you continue like you have been, you will be back in here or in the cemetery. Make your choice."

As Rosie sat in the chair in the doctor's office, her life flashed before her. She started crying as she thought about Blake, George, and John depending on her. She looked at the trusted doctor and told him she could not afford to take off from work. She told him her situation as a single mom trying to make a living for her son and brother. I don't even know how I'm going to pay you. The doctor's demeanor changed from trust to slime. He grabbed her hand again, but this time, instead of holding it, he caressed her hand. With a sly smile he looked at the young, attractive, well-built, black woman and said, "Well, Mrs. Maxwell, maybe we can work out something between the two of us."

As naïve as Rosie was, she understood what he was trying to say. She grabbed her purse and left. Because she was so exhausted it was easy to rest the first week, but by the second week she did a little cleaning and cooking. Thinking of her financial status made her nervous and uneasy.

Callie saw how depressed she was and invited her to a special church service. The next Sunday afternoon, then, George, John, and Rosie joined Callie at **Clouds of Joy Baptist Church**. Rosie tried to brighten her spirits by looking as nice as she possibly could. The black dress she had bought for Blake's funeral looked exceptionally stunning on a woman who was not in mourning.

CHAPTER 11

REVEREND JONES

Reverend Jones was sitting in the pulpit with eight other ministers when she walked in.

He wrote a note to the minister closest to him, "Find out the name of that young woman dressed in black, immediately, please." The note was passed to Reverend Moore's armor bearer who was sitting on the side in the front pew. The armor bearer got up and went to the back of the church and started his search.

The reverend began his sermon: "I want to thank you for the invitation to preach this fine day. It's good to see my fellow ministers from our sister churches and I thank all of you for supporting your minister by attending this special service. Thank you all for coming out on this beautiful day to hear my message. This sermon is not for you sitting in front of me (he pointed to the congregation); this sermon is directed to my esteemed brethren seated in the high seats behind me, my colleagues, my fellow ministers (he turned around and looked at the visiting ministers). Congregation, you must excuse me if I have my back to you during this sermon, but I'll get back to you in just a little while.

"Proverbs 27:23 says, 'Be diligent to know the state of your flocks and look well to your herd. The shepherd must take care of his sheep. Now... now, in another version it says, 'The shepherd must tend to his sheep.' Usually when we talk about the shepherd we are talking about God or Jesus. Today, gentlemen, I want to remind you, as reverends, ministers, pastors, or whatever you call yourselves, you are the shepherds of your congregations. The 23rd Psalm says, 'The Lord is my shepherd I shall not want.' My fellow ministers, you are not the Lord, but you are the shepherd of your flock. The shepherd must lead his sheep to green pastures, beside still waters. He must restore their souls, and when your sheep walk through the valley of the shadow of death, you should be with them."

The minister turned around to the congregation. Two of the ministers let out a sigh of relief.

"My good people, when you go to your house of worship on Sunday morning, it is up to the shepherd to do everything he can in his sermon to lead you to green pastures. The message should be full of what you need. You should feel that you are in a beautiful place, a place that, if you were a sheep, you could get your sustenance. If you come to church feeling depressed and sad, the shepherd should restore your soul. When you leave, the dark clouds should be parted, and your soul should be able to see the sunshine. You should run home to study the Book and hunger for more of that restoration.

"Now, now, that rod and staff that comfort you, you might not like. The shepherd must lead the sheep, but he must do what has to be done to keep the sheep on the straight and narrow. Sometimes the shepherd has to prod the sheep a little. You know, jab him a little to get his attention. Keep them from straying. Now, now, maybe none of you good folks have ever strayed, but if you do, you might get a little prodding." He pushed his arm out as if he jammed someone.

He turned back to the ministers. "You must prepare the table before you. When you take care of the sheep and the sheep follow you, you are anointed, and your cup will run over. But you gotta tend to the sheep. You must know each one of them. You have to listen to them. One sheep might bleat 'BAA' and it means joy, while another sheep might go 'BAA' and it means pain. Know each one of your sheep and tend to your sheep.

"Now, now, it is necessary for the shepherd to do his job if he wants the reward he will receive from his sheep. You know what I mean. At shearing time if you didn't take care of the sheep, some ran that way and some ran the other; a wolf ate one, and one fell into the river and drowned. Brother you ain't gonna have very much wool. Now Ministers, **you** are the shepherds!"

Then he turned and gestured to the congregation, "And **you** are the sheep."

He turned back to the ministers. "It is our responsibility to see that our sheep are well cared for. It is our responsibility to make sure our sheep have what they need so they can give us what we need to do our job as leader of the flock. Now, now, we aren't supposed to do all the work. Now, now, we are the leader, but not the only worker. One sheep spoke up when he saw another sheep wandering off. Elders, Deacons, Mothers of the church, Church school teachers—you know who you are. We all have work to do here. You need to do what you do to help us do what we need to do."

He turned again to the congregation, "Now, now did you hear what I just said? We need you to help do what you do to help us do what you need us to do.

"That's not so hard to understand, is it? Now, now, I'm talking to both sides now," as he turned back and forth with this message.

"When you go to work, all your boss asks of you is to come to work when you are supposed to, do your job when you are there, and go home when you are finished. God is asking you for the same respect."

The reverend paused and waved to the ministers and the congregation, "The only difference is, our work is **never done**! We must keep God's commandments, we must love God and love our neighbor, and we must be fruitful and gather other sheep into our flock. The work is overwhelming, ahh, but it pays back in big rewards. There ain't no paycheck here on earth like the one you gonna receive in heaven.

"We as ministers do not want to overwhelm you, and we as ministers do not want to be overwhelmed. Moses' father-in-law came to him and said, 'Man, you can't solve everybody's problems. You just handle the hard ones and let some good men help you with the easy ones. Even Solomon with all his wisdom got help from the good men around him.' People, don't overload your minister. Help him to do what God wants him to do.

"Now, now, we as shepherds have been given the word of the Lord to give you. We must study and learn the word, we must share the word, and we must feed you with the word. When you want to get out of church early and we keep talking, that's not to hear ourselves talk. It is because we want to be sure when you leave here you have what you need to keep the wolf away, to keep you from straying, and to be fed in the green pastures."

All the ministers in the pulpit were still awake. Normally by now, one or two heads would be bobbing back and forth. They wanted to see where this sermon was going.

"And when you complain that you didn't get anything out of church, look at yourself .... What did you contribute? What did you put into your institution to help make everything work? You just can't sit out there on Sunday morning and expect everybody else is gonna run this operation.

"Come on now ... We **all** gotta help .... You want help? So do the shepherds. We got a sheep laying there on his back that needs help to get up. We got one straying off down in that briar patch that needs help. You know who you are. One getting ready to have a baby needs help, and one just sad and down-hearted needs help. And don't sit there needing help and don't ask 'cause you don't want to bother nobody, or you don't want anybody in your business. Then you get mad 'cause nobody lent a helping hand ... Now, now, come on now. I'm talking for the ministers and the pastors. We need help. You need help. We need your help!

"So, I say SHEPHERDS, tend to your flock, but I also say SHEEP, tend to each other and tend to your SHEPHERD. We can all reap the riches of a good harvest at shearing time. We can all stay warm next season because we did God's will this season."

When the sermon was over, Reverend Jones went to the back of the church to shake everyone's hand as they exited. Rosie was not aware that when he shook her hand, he took a good, long look at her. And while he was shaking the hand of the next person, he was watching Rosie as she walked away.

Life took a U-turn when she returned to work. She tried to take it easy, but she was behind in her rent and utilities and needed to work. One day as she was sweating five pounds off her already slim frame, the ladies in the front of the salon started yelling about the big black Lincoln that pulled up out front. Someone said it looked like Reverend Jones's car. They wondered who he was sniffing around in this neighborhood. The car sat there for about five minutes before the chauffeur slowly exited the car, came into the shop, and asked to see Mrs. Maxwell. The owner, Bessie, directed him to Rosie. The usually noisy shop became quiet as clouds floating in the sky. He approached her and asked if she would come out and have a word with Reverend Jones in his car.

It was hot, it was busy; she was pushing herself to finish five more heads, and she was tired. "Why is this man trying to evangelize me at my job?" She gave him a brief look and continued to wave the head she was working on. The chauffeur stood there waiting for an answer. Rosie let him stand, not looking at him or saying a word.

"Mrs. Maxwell, did you hear me?" he said softly.

She turned her back and continued waving and did not answer. Eventually the chauffeur left. The car sat there for a few minutes, then pulled away.

The next day about the same time the chauffeur was back. He came into the shop and went directly to Rosie. He asked her the same question as he did the day before. Rosie continued to ignore him. This time he waited longer, but he finally left. The shop was quiet when the chauffeur was inside. When he left there was a low murmur. No one said anything to Rosie, but she heard the giggles and whispers.

Two days passed before the chauffeur reappeared. Rosie thought he had given up, but there he was again. Cora yelled from the front of the shop, "Rosie, here comes your boy."

This time before he got to her, she started talking, "Look mister, I'm trying to make a living here, and you're slowing me down. Tell your boss, or whatever he is, that I'm not going to talk to him. I would really appreciate it if he'd leave me alone and let me do my work."

Everyone in the shop heard her.

"Mrs. Maxwell, my boss, as you call him, is a very persistent man. I want you to know I'm as tired of coming in here asking you the same thing over and over as you are hearing it. I know him, and he will not stop until he talks to you face to face in private. So do us both a favor, get it over with. Please give him five minutes of your expensive time."

She grabbed the sweaty towel that she used to wipe her face and marched out to the car and got in.

Reverend Jones sat enthroned in the back seat of the car. He was not an attractive man: short, stubby, partially bald, and dark skinned. He looked shorter in the back of the car than he did when he was preaching in the pulpit. Taking in his expensive suit, huge stylish tie, expensive cologne, and Stacy Adams shoes, spit shined like a mirror, Rosie compared him to herself in her white stained uniform and smelling like the beauty salon.

He started talking as soon as she sat down. The chauffeur started the car and drove away from the shop. The reverend introduced himself and told her he saw her at church on Sunday. Since that time he had been gathering information about her. He knew she was widowed, had a son, and was raising her brother. He also knew that she recently had a nervous breakdown from working too hard.

Rosie 's frown grew deeper. "Mr. Reverend, I have no idea why my personal life is any of your business, and furthermore, Mr. Reverend Jones, according to the agreement I made with your chauffeur, you have approximately three minutes left to tell me why you are pestering the hell out of me. Then I would appreciate it if you'd steer your car back to the beauty shop."

"I will get straight to the point, My Lady." He told her he was looking for a beautiful lady like her to be his companion and escort when he went to important meetings.

Before he could finish the sentence, she scowled. "Is that what this is all about?" She tapped the chauffeur on the shoulder, "No, I'm not playing. Kindly take me back to the shop. Now. Please." She grabbed the towel and wiped her face, sat back and didn't say another word.

The Reverend nodded at the chauffeur to drive her back to the shop. When they drove up, she jumped out before the chauffeur could open the door. She heard the reverend say as she slammed the door, "Think about it, I will make it worth your while."

"Your time is up, leave me alone," she said as she walked to the shop.

Rosie went straight back to her station without looking at anyone or saying a word. Everyone was looking at her as if she were the guest speaker stepping up to the podium. They were disappointed when the closed-mouthed Rosie went back to curling hair.

She heard Cora say, "Um-huh, guess she changed her mind about talking to him."

Rosie still didn't say a word.

At the end of the day while Bessie and Rosie were sweeping and preparing to go home, Bessie said, "Rose, I think I know what the reverend wanted. You want to talk about it?"

Rosie was embarrassed to tell what happened, but she wanted to talk to someone. She told Bessie what he said on the short ride around the block. Bessie continued cleaning and didn't respond for a few minutes. Then she came back and told Rosie to sit down for a minute.

"Honey, I know this is not something you would normally do, but under the circumstances, with your health and financial difficulties, it may be something, at least, to consider. "

Rosie was shocked that Bessie would ask her to even consider being an escort to that man. She seemed to be such a Christian person. The look on her face revealed what she was thinking, but she didn't say another word about it to Bessie or anyone else.

The next week was really busy. Three different ladies came and asked specifically for her. Rosie was waving one head when the lady's son, who was about the same age as George, came in to wait for his mother. He was dressed in seersucker pants, a nice white shirt and tie, and a good-looking pair of shoes. She could not take her eyes off him, wishing she could afford to dress George so fashionably. All day she thought about that young, well-dressed boy. When she finished the last head, she was exhausted and had to rest before she left the shop. Her hands, feet, and legs ached; her head hurt, and she felt a little lightheaded. "Lord, please don't let me have another breakdown." She was so tired she wanted to close her eyes and wish herself home.

It was as hot outside the shop as it was inside. There sat that long Lincoln. As she closed the door behind her the window rolled down and the Reverend said,"Hello, My Lady." He asked her if she would like a ride home. Out of exasperation, heat, and fatigue, Rosie climbed into the car. On the floor was a basin of warm fragrant water for her to soak her feet. The reverend reached down and took off her shoes and massaged her feet through her nylons. While he was rubbing the sore, tired feet he talked in a soft, soothing voice. Rosie took all her troubles from the day, all her aches and pains, wrapped them in a mental trash box, threw them out the window, reared back in the plush backseat, and relaxed.

The reverend was saying something about how he wanted to take care of her and her son. Her ears perked up when he said "Your son."

"Your son will have everything he needs."

Rosie listened, remembering the well-dressed youngster in the shop that day.

"I know how much you love him, and you want the best for him." While talking, he continued to massage her feet and it felt soooo good.

Rosie held her head in her hands looking down and probably did not realize that she was so at ease until that word poured like honey dripping from her mouth, "Ahhhh." She did not see the smile on the reverend's face.

But he knew that, at that moment, he had her.

As she lay in bed alone that night all Rosie could think about was having her feet rubbed. It felt so good, it was like sexless sex. She did not want to be involved with this man in any way, but she was afraid she was letting her guard down. She was a respectful person and all her life she tried to keep her dignity. But there, 'way back in the recesses of her mind, lay the notion of not having to struggle all day, every day; it was like receiving an endowment. That night as she slept, she dreamed of dancing around like a queen on a diamond floor with a gold crown on her head. When she woke up, she tried to shake off all that nonsense. As she left for work, though, she couldn't wipe the smile off her face.

That morning the Lincoln was there. She quietly got into the car, still not looking at the reverend. He handed her a jewelry box and asked her to open it. Inside was what appeared to be a beautiful diamond pin. She handed it back to him and told him she could not take it. "Mrs. Maxwell, I owe you this. I've been harassing you for the last two weeks. I want to apologize with this gift. Yes, it is diamonds, and yes, it is expensive, and yes you are more beautiful and worth more than this pin. Please take it, even if you never want to see me again. I just ask you to think about my proposal. I'll not pressure you anymore."

"But you won't regret spending time with me. All I will ask from you is to go places with me and be as beautiful as you are. I will not force you to do anything you do not want to do. I will give you everything you need to be the lady I want to be with. I only ask you to consider my request until I see you again. Mrs. Maxwell, I am very attracted to you. The car will be at the shop to take you home whenever you want. I have some business to attend to and will not see you for a while. I'll communicate with you through the chauffeur." The car stopped at the shop. Rosie quickly stuck the jewelry box in her purse and watched as the Lincoln drove away.

After Rosie gave in and allowed the chauffeur to drive her to and from work, her life changed. She didn't see or hear from the reverend, but she asked the driver to come every day. The second day he told her the reverend had sent something for her that he had to carry to her apartment. He opened the trunk to reveal bags filled with all kinds of groceries, meat, vegetables, dairy products—enough to last the family for two weeks.

Three days later there was an elegant, wrapped package laying on the back seat. The chauffeur told her it was for her from the reverend. She opened it to find a book of poems and a hundred-dollar bill as a bookmark. This new Rose was sucked into a higher class of living with a gust of unstoppable gifts lavished on her almost daily. The old Rose who scrimped and saved every penny to make ends meet was escorted away to a distant place. She was not there when Rosie stood in front of the mirror with her diamond pin on her lapel. The new woman took George and John shopping for new, store-bought clothes. She felt a load lift off that made her feel ten pounds lighter and ten years younger.

Weeks passed without seeing the reverend, but he continued to send the gifts; some were costly, others were thoughtful. She looked forward to getting into the car to see what surprise was waiting for her. At first she didn't miss seeing her benefactor, but there was a longing in the back of her mind to see him. Each day she thought that might be the day he returned. She never asked the chauffeur about him. They talked about other things.

She had some interesting conversations with the chauffeur during that time. His name was Barry; he was married with two children. They were teenagers now, but he was trying to pressure them to go to college. His mother-in-law lived with them and helped take care of the children while he and his wife worked. They talked about their children, home life, politics, and sometimes religion. They became friends, laughing and talking on the short ride to and from work.

And then one day the reverend was back. On a cold blustery day in November as she happily scrambled to get inside the warm car, there he was.

Nervously, she looked up to see him. Since she had become comfortable with Barry, the reverend's presence was almost an intrusion, but he had a way of making everything work his way. He started by talking small talk, asking about her health, her job, and her family. He never asked about the gifts he sent.

When they got to her place, he told her he wanted to talk to her for a minute. He asked Barry to take a walk. Rosie got nervous. He grabbed her hand, looked in her eyes and in his soft calm voice he told her he wanted to make some changes in her life. This place you live is so small. I have looked into another apartment for your family. Barry will take you to see it, if you agree. After you move, I would like you to go on a short vacation with me.

Rosie's heart started to race and so did her thoughts, *Move? Vacation? Move where? What is a vacation? Go somewhere? Oh, oh what 's going on now?*

"I can't leave her son and brother," she stammered. Maybe she was getting in over her head.

The minister was way ahead of her. "Take your time, Mrs. Maxwell. The chauffeur will take you to see the apartment. Don't worry about the rent, that's all been taken care of. That is, if you like it. I might like to visit you sometime, and I can't do so in that kitchenette where you live now. Please consider it.

"In a month I'm going to Chicago for some business, and there will be a prize fight that same weekend. I'd like you to go with me. I have a housekeeper who'll stay with your young men. I wish you'd think about all of this. I know this is a lot to throw on you at one time, but I've been looking for a place I thought you and your family might like. Take your time before you answer. Let Barry know."

Rosie looked out the window at Barry walking around outside on this very cold, snowy day. *It's awfully cold for Barry to be walking around out there*, she thought.

The reverend read her thoughts, "Barry's OK; he won't freeze to death. That would be you if you didn't allow me to give you a ride."

She stiffened at that statement. She shifted away from the reverend and looked out at Barry pacing back and forth, stamping his feet.

"I like that about you, My Lady, you are a very caring person." He reached over the seat and tooted the horn for Barry to come back to the car. Before he climbed in, Barry went around to the trunk and took out a box that Rosie knew would be another gift for her.

She touched the ribbon but didn't open the glossy box.

When Barry opened her door so she could get out of the car, the reverend told her Barry would show her the apartment after she got off from work the next day. "Think about everything I said. I'll get back to you, My Lady."

She took the box straight to her room and put it under the bed unopened and fixed dinner for the boys. After they were asleep she opened the box and almost fainted. On top of the tissue paper a note read the words Blake had said to her years ago, "I think this will look good on you." She pulled back the tissue paper and took out a blue dress. THE BLUE DRESS! As well as she could remember, this dress was so close in design to the dress she had longed for back in Macon, Georgia. The dress she destroyed when Papa gave it to her sister. Her heart was beating so fast. How did he know? Was this a coincidence? She sat down and hugged the dress and cried. She finally had her blue dress. Rosie could not know, then, that this was not the last blue dress she would receive.

George woke up when he heard his mother crying and came to her room to see if she was sick. "What's wrong, Mommy?"

At first, she couldn't stop crying to answer him. When she got herself together she said, "Oh, baby, nothing is wrong; everything is very good. Tell me, how would you like to move into a new apartment?"

George and John had their own rooms in the new apartment. The kitchen was as large as the kitchenette that everyone had shared in the old apartment. Her large bedroom was on the corner of the building with a window on the west and south sides. The reverend had all her furniture moved into the apartment, and he bought new beds for the boys. The day they moved in, a huge bouquet of roses was on the table. There was an envelope with money for her to buy anything else she needed. Three days later Barry brought the elderly housekeeper over for her approval. Mrs. Yaw won everyone's hearts with the box of homemade cookies she brought.

Afterwards, all the arrangements were completed for the trip. The boys didn't understand what was going on, but they were happy to have their own bedroom and a lady to stay who baked cookies for them. Mrs. Yaw came a day before the trip, while Rosie was there, so she could get used to the place. She was a pleasant, motherly type and easy to get along with. Rosie felt comfortable leaving her kids with this lady.

As she was making her last preparations, Rosie answered a telephone call from a voice she did not recognize. Something was familiar but so far away. Finally, she got it–Brent! "Where are you? Are you here in town? Oh, I'm so glad to hear your voice." She heard happy tears in her voice.

He told her he was not ready to tell his family just yet. Then, Brent asked, "I heard that you have a "sorta" boyfriend? Don't ask me how I knew." During the phone call, Brent never told Rosie where he was. She wondered, but she didn't want to pry. She learned later that nobody in the family knew where he was.

"It's so good to hear your voice Rosie; I might send you a picture one day…love you Sister! Goodbye." And just like that, Brent was gone.

"How many years until I see him again?" she whispered. She was so happy to hear from her brother she let the tears flow. She was thinking about a lot of things from their childhood. Thinking aloud, she asked herself, "What am I doing, and where am I going? What should I do?"

Then the doorbell rang and in came the Reverend.

Seeing the reverend right after the call with her brother sent her mind racing. "Everything is not good. Some things are great, and others are bad! What am I doing with my life?" she whispered to herself while moving forward to greet the reverend.

The reverend, his usual pleasant self, offered her a gift of flowers and chocolates.

But Rosie couldn't stop thinking to herself: *Sometimes I want to be home and other times I can't wait to see new places. I give, I take…sometimes I just want to scream! In my life I have old folks, young folk, even children, but what can I do to help somebody…anybody? What did somebody do to help me make. . . me? Why do I just want to scream? I need help. I got help. WHERE, WHAT, WHO, SHOULD I, CAN I… .*

Rosie kept all these thoughts to herself. She knew things weren't quite right with her life. Still, she thanked the reverend for the flowers and chocolate, and they had a nice visit.

CHAPTER 12

THE GOOD LIFE

The day of the big trip finally arrived. She had never been on a vacation or to Chicago. The reverend asked her to wear the blue dress, but not to bring anything else. She couldn't figure out why, but she followed orders.

Barry drove them to Chicago. The ride was smooth but quiet with very little conversation. Rosie was apprehensive and a little bewildered about what he would expect from her. Their quarters were at a private house. The housekeeper showed her to her room. The reverend went in with her. He told her right away that his room was down the hall. He added, "I bought a few things for you. Open the closet."

She was amazed to see a closet full of new clothes. She took out a suit to check the size. Perfect! Each outfit had coordinated shoes, purse, and hat. He directed her to the dresser. There were scarves, jewelry, and perfume. All the toiletries that she would need were there also.

"Breakfast is served at eight o'clock," began the reverend. "If you want anything for lunch, they will have sandwiches in the kitchen. Barry will take you anywhere you want to go. I'll be gone all day for a business meeting, but I'll pick you up at 4:00 pm for dinner, and then we'll go to the fight. I hope you wear that gray suit. I think you'll look fabulous in it, but I think you look fabulous in everything. I'll have your coat brought up to you later." He took her hand.

Rosie trembled as she thought, *Oh, Oh, here we go. This is when he expects me to pay up.*

The reverend moved in close and looked in her eyes and said, "My

Lady, I really appreciate your company. Thank you." He kissed her on the cheek and left.

After he left, she tried on every outfit in the closet with the shoes, blouses, purses, and jewelry. Everything fit! How did he know? It was as if the clothes were made for her.

On Friday, they went to dinner and the fight. Each day after that they spent sightseeing at a different Chicago landmark. It was a whirlwind weekend with money spent like Rosie never saw in her life. On Saturday, the reverend met her at breakfast and told her the agenda for that day. He would go to his business meetings and return about three o'clock, and they would leave by four. He would come to her room and pick her up. At the end of the day, he escorted her back to her room and went away. She didn't know what she was going to do when and if he tried to sleep with her, but he never tried.

When they were out, he gave her all his attention. Anything she wanted to eat or drink or see, he saw that she was accommodated. They had long conversations and he listened intently to what she said. She thought, *Who could be interested in my life as a widowed hairdresser raising two kids?* But he seemed to be. She laughed more than she had laughed since Blake was alive. She danced in the beautiful dresses and shoes that he bought her. Her soul was happy. That was a feeling she had not felt for a long time.

The drive home was relaxing and enjoyable. The three of them in the big Lincoln laughed and talked all the way, reminiscing about the things that happened that weekend. The reverend told her he had never enjoyed himself as much as he did on this trip. He said it was such a joy to be out with a beautiful, dignified, refined lady. He told her the housekeeper could stay as long as she wanted her.

At her apartment the reverend got out and walked her to the door and thanked her for agreeing to go with him. "I hope you had as good of a time as I did. I know you missed some days of work so here is enough to make up for it." He gave her an envelope with more money than she would have made in a month. When they got to the door of her apartment, he kissed her and just then George opened the door. That was the first time they had seen each other. What George saw, he didn't like. The reverend introduced himself to George and said, "Goodnight, My Lady." He went back to the car and sent Barry up with the luggage.

The first trip to Chicago was exciting, but the next trip to Ontario was better. Rosie spent the days with two other ladies who came with their minister friends. They shopped and dined until evening when their beaus met them for dinner. After dinner they saw a stage show, Rosie's first, and then went to a nightclub. About every other month there was a vacation or short trip, some close, some farther away.

Her days at the beauty shop started to dwindle to a few days a week. At first, Bessie told her not to worry about the snakes-in-the-grass, "Everyone in here talks about everyone else in here when they aren't here. So, know that when you are gone, you're fair game!"

Rosie did not mind the talk when she was gone, but she hated the looks and whispers when she was there. The only reason she had continued to go to the shop was to have some cloak of income so no one would know the reverend was totally supporting her. Eventually, it was hardly worthwhile: She stopped going to the shop. She didn't need the money, and the sneers of the other women had become more than she could handle.

She saw the reverend seldom and they did not have a routine. Weeks would pass and she heard nothing from him. Rosie never complained or let him know she was anxious to see him. She waited patiently for a call or a visit. She accommodated him when he showed up.

When the phone rang, she was happy to hear his voice, "Hello, My Lady, how are you?

You have no idea how much I've missed you. Do you have time to spend with me this afternoon? I'll bring groceries"

Even though they had been a couple for over a year, Rosie felt her heart skip whenever he called or came over. She wondered if she was actually in love or if she was just gratefully living a lifestyle she truly enjoyed. And every now and then the feeling of guilt came upon her. With all the happiness she received, she knew it was sinful. She was caught in a quagmire; she took one day at a time and she never stopped praying asking for mercy and forgiveness.

He brought steaks and potatoes and applesauce. While they were eating the telephone rang. Rosie was shocked that the phone rang twice in one day. She received very few calls and usually it was the reverend calling, but he was here. She picked up the phone and was surprised to hear her sister, Mardine, calling from Cleveland.

It had to be something very important for the family to call long distance, it was too expensive. Rosie was apprehensive thinking something was wrong with her parents. Rosie had not heard from anyone since the letter she got from her mother two weeks earlier telling her that Papa was moving to Cleveland.

In a nervous voice she shouted, "Is everyone OK?"

"Calm down, Rosie. We are all good. We just have a problem that I'm asking everyone to help resolve. You know I can't talk long, and I know you don't have a lot to give, but I am collecting money from all the sisters and brothers. Papa agreed to move to Cleveland from Macon and he bought a house. Not long after they moved in, the furnace died. I am trying to offset the cost by collecting from everybody. If you can help, even a little, just send it to this address."

Rosie got a pencil and wrote down the new address of her father and mother. "Yes, Mardine, I promise to send something soon as I can."

Mardine asked, "Why are you home? Off day from the shop?"

Rosie tensed, "Why did you call if you thought I would not be home?"

Mardine heard something in her voice that she did not understand. "What's up with you? I just asked. OK, send what you can, bye."

Two weeks later Mardine called again and asked Rosie about her contribution. Rosie told her she sent $25.00. Then, Mardine asked if she knew who sent the money to pay for the whole furnace?

"I am so happy that it's paid for, but I can't figure out who has enough money to pay it out right. You know me, Rosie, I won't stop snooping until I find out who paid for it. Everyone I called was struggling and barely could send what you sent."

Four days passed before Mardine called back; her voice sounded strangely calm. She asked Rosie how everything was at the beauty shop.

"Mardine, why are you asking me all these questions?" Rosie's voice sharpened.

Mardine softly said, "Rosie, I've heard rumors about you that I don't want to believe. I'm calling you so you can tell me the truth."

Rosie, shaking nervously, sat down. She had not mentioned her lifestyle to anyone in the family.

Mardine continued, "I talked to John yesterday and he told me about the reverend and your lavish lifestyle. "Rosie, I called Sears & Roebuck and asked who paid for the furnace; they wouldn't tell me. I don't know anyone in this family who has that kind of money, it could only come from HIM," Mardine snarled.

The way she said HIM sounded to Rosie the same way she used to say "Yellow Rose." Then her voice turned sweet and kind, "Rosie don't do this to yourself. Don't let Satan control your life. What kind of example are you setting for George and John? If you need to pack up and come home, then come, but don't lower yourself to be a kept woman. You are now messing with God. Please read Proverbs, Chapters Eight and Nine and consider what you are doing. We don't want this furnace. I am going to call Sears and tell them to take it back."

Before Rosie could respond, Mardine hung up.

She sat down and tried to think this one out. Could the reverend have paid for the furnace? How did he know? *I never told him about this. I would never ask him to do something like that. What's going on here?* Then she remembered that when Mardine called, the reverend had been there with the steaks for lunch. Mardine said she would keep snooping until she found out.

"I can't believe she made two long distance calls in one month!" mumbled Rosie. Her brain felt like scrambled eggs. Too much to sort out. *How am I going to explain my lifestyle to the family? Oh, that Mardine probably interrogated John until she got all the information she was looking for. She's done it before.*

The telephone rang again. Mardine was yelling at the top of her voice, "Papa made me call you back and tell you to tell that man thank you for the furnace. If I had my way, we would throw it in the lake. I would rather freeze all winter long than be warmed by the fires of hell."

She slammed down the phone again.

Three long distance calls in one month, Rosie thought. *Wow!*

Rosie still had many unanswered questions only the reverend could answer. Since she never called him, she had to wait for him to get in touch with her before she could ask him about the furnace. One afternoon, not long after Mardine's call, they enjoyed a dinner of fried chicken, collard greens, and candied sweet potatoes that Rosie prepared.

After the meal, she asked him about the furnace. "I want to ask you if you did it and if so, how? How did you know about it? How did you know who and where to send it, and why did you do it?"

"Whoa, whoa, My Lady, that's a lot of questions to ask a man who just finished a huge, delicious meal like I just ate. Sit down and relax a minute. Give my food a chance to digest before we get into that."

And Rosie sat.

He had a way of controlling situations and seemed to be collecting his words before he spoke, "My Lady, whenever you have a chance to be a blessing to someone, do it. I saw a need, I had the resources, and I did it. I didn't do it because they were your parents. I did it because they needed a furnace, and I could afford to buy them one. I've done the same for other people. I didn't tell you because sometimes it's good to keep things between yourself and God. You become a light shining in the darkness. God will bless you and others. The blessings go far, deep, and wide.

CHAPTER 13

HE LOVES ME... HE LOVES ME NOT... HE....

The reverend called and asked her to bring a picnic basket with everything but the food. He would bring that. We are going to the country for a quiet afternoon picnic. This was not their first picnic in the five years they had been together. Many summer afternoons were spent in areas Rosie never knew existed, not that far from her home. They drove for about an hour into the beautiful green countryside. The day was perfect for a picnic. The sky was the bluest blue without a cloud to be seen. They stopped near a small stream that had daisies growing beside it. The water was running over large rocks making a splashing sound. The smell of the fresh air, the beautiful flowers in bloom, the rolling hills and open space added to the ambience of the day.

He brought a large basket with fried chicken, potato salad, lemonade, and a chocolate cake. While Rosie put the food out and fixed the plates, the reverend picked a bunch of flowers and made a bouquet. He brought them to her and said, "If only these flowers were as lovely and sweet as you, My Lady." Rosie blushed and felt joyful all over.

The food was delicious. After they ate, the chauffeur, Rosie, and the reverend laughed, talked, and relaxed. The reverend left to relieve himself, and Rosie talked to the chauffeur about his son going to college. The chauffeur told her the reverend was helping him pay for his son's education.

Rosie remembered his words, "If you have a chance to be a blessing to someone you should do it." The reverend returned and the chauffeur walked away.

Their life together for the last five years had been so exciting. The trips, the gifts, the money, the support, and the surprises had made her life wonderful. Everything she wanted or needed was provided for her. There was the time when her son, George, was caught stealing, and the police called Rosie from the juvenile detention home. Rosie did not call the reverend, but he called her as she was preparing to go for George. The minister told her to stay home, and he would take care of everything. Within an hour George was home. As a result of a long talk between the reverend and the young man, George decided to join the army.

Rosie appreciated all the things he did for her, but she did not crowd him. She never called, she did not visit his church, and she never asked for anything. He had an uncanny sense and he provided her with everything she needed and more. He paid her rent, utilities, bought her clothes, jewelry, and gave her money. He saw to it that she always had enough food in the house. If the weather was bad, she had only to give the chauffeur the grocery list and food was delivered to her apartment.

Through all the years they had been together he only mentioned sex once. She refused him, but secretly wanted him to persist more than he did. That was the last time the subject was mentioned. He kissed her, he hugged her, he rubbed and massaged her feet and he held her close, but that was as far as it went. There were many times when she felt he wanted her, but he never brought it up or mentioned it again. She always respected him for respecting her. As complete as their relationship was, she did not know whether it would be any better if they had been intimate.

The reverend lay with his head on Rosie's lap. She took the bouquet of daisies and pulled out a couple stems. Rosie leaned back on a tree and looked up and saw a bird slowly gliding gracefully through the sky in swoops and circles above them. She watched it for a while thinking how peaceful the bird looked. After a while she asked the reverend to look at the bird. He had been resting with his eyes closed and had to focus to see the bird slowly and elegantly riding the current.

Rosie asked him, "Do you think they fly to get from one point to another or are they flying for enjoyment?"

The minister looked at the bird and then at Rosie. He replied .... "Hmmm, I don't know

about all birds, but I think **that** bird looked down and saw a beautiful lady and thought, 'What can I do to thank her for sharing her beauty? The trees are standing in their splendor waving their arms and clapping their hands. The grass has knit a beautiful carpet for her to lie on.' So, he decided to gently perform to the symphony of the wind for your pleasure. Watch him and thank God for sending him to entertain you."

Rosie was thinking about what he said. She liked to hear the sweet words that were like poetry. She was so comfortable and so relaxed she leaned back and started pulling the petals from the daisy. Softly she said to herself, *He loves me, he loves me not*, all the while wishing this day would never end. She pulled another petal, *He loves me, he loves me not. . . .*

Suddenly the reverend sat up. The look on his face was serious, almost grave. "My Lady, I have to talk to you about something." The mood of the day darkened.

"What's wrong?"

He took a long deep breath and began talking like he was in the pulpit. His words sounded rehearsed, "My Lady, I am so grateful for the relationship we have. You know my commitment is first to God, then to my wife and family, then to my church. I know our relationship is not godly, not right"....

Rosie was still pulling the petals from the daisy, ...*he loves me not*....

He continued, "I am not a perfect man in a lot of ways. When we first met, you said you would not be sexual with me. That was not what I wanted to hear, but I admired you so much and I respected you. I just wanted to be with you."

"With you, I have peace and comfort. You do not ask me for anything, you gratefully accept what I give you. I admire your beauty, grace, and class."

. . . He loves me not; he loves me . . . .

"Even though I'm a powerful minister, I am short, bald, black, and ugly. When I have you on my arm, I feel like Joe Louis. I see the way other men envy me when I am with you. I feel like I am six feet tall."

"I can't tell you that I love you because that would be against my policy, but I'll tell you that being with you is something that keeps me doing all the other things I need to do to be who I am. You would be surprised by all the turmoil I have been able to tolerate just because I think about my time with you–my bad times just melt away. Everywhere I turn people are pulling, nagging, or demanding something from me. Many times, I sit and listen to some absurd wife complaining about her husband. Or the deacons are upset because I didn't acknowledge some minute act. All the while I see your face; I can sit there and smile and know that when I get through this, I'll call you and everything will be alright."

Rosie knew he was going to say something she did not want to hear ..... she continued to slowly pull the petals ...*he loves me* . . . .

"Now, now, My Lady .... My life is about to change. I can't go into detail at this time, but please have patience with me. I may not be able to contact you for quite a while. Please know that you will be on my mind everyday "

She picked the last petal, . . *He loves me not.*

Rosie was trying to hold back the tears, but there they were. It sounded as if he were telling her goodbye. She could not imagine life without him. She dared not ask any questions. She hoped he would give her more information, but he said very little on the ride home. Even though she tried to lighten the mood, the heaviness hung over the three as they rode down the beautiful country road, which a few hours ago had been sunlit, but now had a dark cloud over it.

Weeks passed and she did not see him or hear his voice. Her imagination had been working overtime. Was he sick? Was something going on in his church? Was there a problem with his home life? Every so often she received money or gifts from him, which made her think everything was alright. Maybe he just didn't want to see her anymore. She was alone and lonely. George was in the army, and she very seldom heard from him. Her brother John had married and moved out. She only saw him and his family when they came to dinner on Sunday.

Then one day, six weeks after the picnic, Barry came to her apartment and asked if he could come in and talk to her. She could feel the tension and her knees began to buckle. Barry delivered distressing news, "The reverend wants you to know before it hits the paper, that Mrs. Jones died at four o'clock this morning."

A million thoughts started going through her head. "What can I do for him? How can I console him? Does he need me? And then, what does this mean to our relationship?"

Barry told her not to call the reverend and not to go to the funeral. "The reverend said he will be in touch with you," Barry said with finality, excused himself and left.

The newspaper had a full-page spread of the funeral. Ministers and their wives from all over the country attended the event. She recognized some of the ministers from the many trips she had taken with the reverend. Mrs. Jones had been sick for more than a year, yet had continued to serve as the First Lady of the church until she was too sick to leave the house. The article told of all the wonderful things Mrs. Jones did for her family, the community, the church, and the Lord. She had been a loyal, faithful wife and mother, and she had spent every free minute in the church making sure all was in order for her husband. She helped other wives and nurtured new wives and mothers. She started missionary programs to help the poor and needy in her community. She had been loved by many.

Rosie did not dare attend the funeral. She could not even talk to anyone about it. She stayed home grieving for the man she had given the last five years of her life to while he grieved for the death of his wife. She still received an allowance every month for rent, utilities, and food. The days passed and she heard nothing from him. She never called him, and even though he no longer had a wife, she still respected his space. So, she waited, and waited, and waited. *Maybe this is the end. But why? Now he is a free man, we could be together legally*, she thought.

Finally he called her and apologized for not being in touch for so long. When she asked him how he was doing he sounded as if he was still grieving. He told her he was not doing well and that he missed his wife. For over an hour he spilled out his heart about how wonderful she had and how much he had loved her. He talked about the great mother she was to their children and what a role model she was as the First Lady of the church. The conversation was uncomfortable to Rosie, but she felt his pain and was happy that he felt he could talk to her about anything, even his deceased wife.

"Can you come over?" she asked him. "I need to see you, touch you, hold you, and look you in your eyes. I need to help you in any way I can."

He hesitated a long time before he said anything. Finally, she heard him clear his throat. He told her he could not see her yet. He said he would see her, but not now. "I have a major project to do. I hope you have everything you need ... Now, now, My Lady, I will be in touch with you soon. Goodbye." And he hung up.

Four months had passed since Mrs. Jones' death and Rosie had not seen the reverend once. She was listening to her soap opera on the radio when the phone rang.

"Hello, how are you, My Lady?" his voice rumbled through the receiver.

They had their back-and-forth small talk; then he asked her if he could come over.

She was shocked when she saw him. He didn't look like himself. His clothes hung off him and his eyes were sad. And he was very nervous. Inviting her to sit down, he sat beside her and took her hand. "My Lady, I am a minister of a large church, and it is important that I have a good strong lady beside me, a first lady for the church and a mother for my children. I've taken this time away from you to search my mind and ask the Lord for guidance and direction. I cannot live alone. I need a wife. I've been looking for the perfect lady to replace my wife. I've found the perfect woman; I am planning on marrying her next month."

At first Rosie thought he was talking about her. Then as he kept talking, she realized he was marrying someone else. "I wanted you to be the first... ."

Rosie heard nothing; she fainted. The last thing she remembered was the reverend saying he was getting married. When she revived, the telephone was ringing, the minister was gone, and the envelope with her monthly stipend was on the table.

For the first time since their relationship started, she realized what she was. Even though she refused to have sex with the reverend, she was his concubine. He needed her for all the wrong things. A dry lump scratched the back or her throat, but she could not cry. The telephone was ringing, and she leaped for it, thinking it might be the reverend.

CHAPTER 14

GEORGE COMES HOME

She grabbed the phone, but before she could answer she heard, "Mom, where were you? I'm coming home. See you in two days. Fix me some chicken. And guess what mom? I'm getting married! You remember Little Roxie that I brought over the last time I was home. Well, she's pregnant, and I'm going to do the right thing and marry her. I think I love her; she's real cute. This may be what I need to do to settle down. I probably won't re-up. I'll come home, get a job, and be a good husband. No more wild George."

He was talking so fast she had trouble keeping up.

She tried to take all this in. Her son's getting married, a grandbaby on the way, Little Roxie to be her daughter-in-law.

George kept on talking, trying hard to convince his mom that everything was going to be okay. "We'll get an apartment not far from you and you can see the baby whenever you want, and we'll be one big, happy family," he almost babbled with joy.

As George talked and talked and talked, Rosie began to wonder who he was trying to convince. As his news began to sink in, she started computing: "How far along is Roxie in her pregnancy?" she interrupted

George did not know, only that the baby was due in about three months.

"And son, how long ago did you meet her?"

"When I was home six months ago."

When she went to the bus station to meet George, Rosie could hardly believe how much he looked like a man and how little he looked like her young son.

Before they went home, he wanted to see Little Roxie who lived with her mother on the other side of town.

When Rosie walked into their very small apartment she saw a very pregnant woman. Either the baby was going to be very, very large or she was due to deliver at any moment. Rosie was introduced to Little Roxie and her mother. She smiled and tried to ask questions without appearing nosy. Little Roxie was so glad to see George; she "oooo'd and ahhed" all over him like he was the best thing since sliced bread. She could not keep her hands off him. And George was loving all the attention.

Finally, Rosie asked when the baby was due. Little Roxie's mother twisted her face and stammered, "Not-not for- four– four months!"

Hairs rising on the back of her neck, Rosie turned beet-red. She rose from the end of the couch where she was sitting close to the mother. She looked directly at Little Roxie. In a stern voice she said, "You, Little Roxie, and your mother, are both damn liars!"

George's large eyes widened even more as he looked at his mother–the words from her mouth he had never heard before.

Rosie moved closer to LIttle Roxie, "You know this is not George's baby. You are at least nine months pregnant, and George was not home eight or nine months ago."

Turning back to the mother, she hissed, "You obviously are looking for a paycheck for this little bastard and a husband for this hussy. Well, I am here to tell you it is not going to be my son!"

She turned and looked at George, "Let's get the hell out of here."

George stood still with the look of total amazement on his face. His huge eyes bugged out as he looked at his mother, Little Roxie, and her mother. Little Roxie started to cry, and she clung to George tighter than she had been. She was yelling that it was his baby, 'cause he was the only man she had ever slept with.

Little Roxie's mother jumped up and stood in front of the door. "Who do you think you calling a hussy? At least me or my daughter ain't sleeping with a man of God. You think you are Miss High-and-Mighty. Everyone knows what you are and being a hussy would be ten steps UP for you. And this son of yours who don't have enough backbone to stand up for himself!"

Little Roxie's mother shooed her hands away like she was scaring away geese. "He had to bring his mommy to help him. I heard he's been sleeping around so much, he don't know where he left all his babies. You better not throw a stone in the schoolyard, Missy, 'cause you just might hit one of his kids. Now you get the hell out of my house you phony, sinful bitch."

Rosie retorted, "Don't try to take the focus off your daughter and that baby. They are the main attraction at this event. And what does that show for you? If you thought that my son was such a scoundrel, why would you want that kind of man to marry your daughter? I know it's not him you want, but that army allotment check. I see who put her up to this deception. I don't think she is that deceitful or that smart. But you. . . you . . . How desperate are you? Now, if you want to talk about me, come to my arena and we can have our own bout. What I think you better do now is go out and try to find out who the baby's daddy is, cause it ain't my son."

She grabbed George and yanked him away from Little Roxie and out of the apartment and almost pushed him down the steps. He did not resist.

George spent most of his time at home in bars and out with his friends. The argument at Little Roxie's was hard on him. He was ashamed because he thought the baby was his. He did not even think that she could have been already pregnant when they were together. What Little Roxie's mother said about his mother was hard on him too. He knew his mother was having an affair with the reverend, but he did not know everyone knew about it. And to hear his mother curse was a shock to him. So for the rest of his furlough, he avoided her as much as possible, and when it was time to leave he was glad to go.

Rosie was hanging clothes on the line when she heard the phone ring. She hoped it was the reverend. She had not heard from him since the day he told her he was getting married. Her mind was still in turmoil. He never defined their relationship. He told her he could not say he loved her, but she was sure he did. When his first wife died, she thought they would become closer; she never thought that he would marry someone else! She thought of him a lot and cried. She had no idea what was to become of her and their relationship. She ran into the house; just as she picked up the receiver, she heard the click. *Oh well, I guess they'll call back if it's important.* She hoped George was not calling long distance. She hoped it was the reverend.

She started back outside and the phone rang again; this time she grabbed it. She heard, "Hello, Mrs. Maxwell?

"Yes this is she."

"How are you today?"

"Fine, who's calling please?"

"Why, Mrs. Maxwell, this is the new Mrs. Jones. I thought you and I needed to have a talk so there will be no misunderstanding between us."

Rosie's heart started beating like crazy, she started to tremble. Why was this woman calling her? She had not seen the reverend since his new marriage. Yes, she still received a monthly allowance, and she was hoping one day she would see the minister, but they had not communicated in any way since he told her he was getting married.

Rosie could not talk. She held the phone waiting to hear what this woman wanted to say. She was probably going to cuss her out like Little Roxie's mother did.

"Mrs. Maxwell, are you there?"

She managed to get the words out, "Yes, I'm here."

"Mrs. Maxwell, I want you to know that the arrangement you had with the ex-Mrs. Jones you will not have with me. I heard that she said she respected you because you never disrespected her or her family by showing up in church or anywhere near her or her family. Well, I want you to know you will not disrespect me by being anywhere near my husband or you will be sorry. The arrangement you had with my husband is over. And, Mrs. Maxwell, I mean totally over."

Rosie heard the reverend's voice in the background asking her who she was talking to. The phone clicked off.

The phone rang again. She did not answer. She could not talk to that woman again. The phone rang and rang. Afraid that it might be George, she picked up the phone and heard the reverend. He spoke softly. "I apologize for what you just had to go through."

Rosie wanted to hang up, but she was so glad to hear his voice. She started to cry. As he was talking, she could no longer hear what he was saying; her heart was hurting and her body trembling. With effort, she took a deep breath and told him, "Your wife is right. Please do not call me, get in touch with me, or send me anything. I will send anything back if you do. It is time that I start my life without you. Tell your wife I said thank you for helping me see the light."

She heard a click on the line, someone had picked up an extension, then she heard him say, "Wait, wait I need to tell you..." and she hung up.

She had some money saved, not enough to last for a long time. Now she had to get a job. Her new life was about to begin. *Well*, she thought, *I guess I am out of the sun and back into the clouds.*

CHAPTER 15

MOMMIE

There were no tears. Crying didn't help. A new life was about to begin, and she had no idea where to start. For the last six years she had lived the life of a kept woman, wanting for nothing. George was in the army; her brother and his family had moved to Cleveland. She was the most alone and lonely she had ever been. Her jumbled mind held not one clear thought.

It was two o'clock in the morning. She had been sitting at the dining room table staring into space for hours. "Help me Lord!" It felt good just voicing words. She had not spoken out loud for two days. She said it again, "Help me Lord."

Coherent thoughts came into her head. She got a pencil and paper and started to write.

> *These things are for sure: You must get yourself together, so you do not have another breakdown. Swallow your pride. You have to get a job. You cannot go back to doing hair in a beauty shop. Call every friend you have and ask if they have an idea where you can find a job.*

She took her list and put it under her pillow and went to bed. That night she was able to sleep. The first thing the next morning she started calling everyone friend, cousin, and acquaintance about a job. Rosie still did hair at her apartment for a few of her friends. So, when Gladys came on Saturday, Rosie shocked her by asking for employment information. Gladys told her she would ask around. The next morning she got up early and went to the bus stop. Many days when she rode in the big black Lincoln, she had seen ladies waiting for the bus to take them to the white ladies' houses to do day work. She approached two ladies and told them she was desperate to find work. They told her they would keep her in mind if they heard of anything. She gave them her telephone number. The next morning she went to another bus stop, continuing every morning until she got a positive answer.

She approached a lady sitting with her stocking rolled down around her ankles and her head tied in a scarf. She had the typical large bag that usually contained a change of clothes and lunch. She had a scowl on her face as if to say, "Leave me alone." Rosie went up to her anyway and asked her if she knew of anybody that needed someone to clean.

"Yeah, I do, but she is so mean, I wouldn't send a dog to her. How desperate are you?" Rosie took the lady's name and went home and called her. The woman sounded mean over the phone. After asking Rosie a lot of questions about her personal life, she told her to come to her house so she could see what she looked like.

Rosie worked for Mrs. Collings for thirteen months. During that entire time she never saw Mrs. Collings smile or say a friendly word. She never heard a "Thank you or I'm sorry. Mrs. Collings very seldom left the house when Rosie was there. She followed her from room to room and watched her as she worked. If she had to leave for an appointment, she had someone come over to watch, to make sure Rosie did not steal anything. The house was a mess when Rosie started to work for her. There was so much clutter everywhere it was difficult to clean. It took Rosie months to clean up so she could clean up. Each day when she returned Mrs. Collings made a new mess for her to get rid of.

Mrs. Collings did not pay much, but it was enough for her to pay her bills and buy food. At this time of her life Rosie was numb to everything except what she had to do to make it through each day. She worked, went home, kept house, and went to bed. She did not socialize, did not go to church, and did not leave the house unless it was absolutely necessary. She could not shake the depression. When she was alone, she sat at the dining room table and stared into space. For 13 months, this was her routine.

Then one Wednesday morning she arrived at Mrs. Collings house with her bag of change of clothes and lunch. Before she could ring the bell, the door was pulled open by a woman who looked like Mrs. Collings, only younger and, if possible, meaner.

"What do you want?" Rosie told her who she was and expected to be let in to do her daily duties. "My mother died during the night. We no longer need your services." The daughter did not ask her in; she said her speech and slammed the door. She did not even pay Rosie for the two days she owed her.

Rosie stood there. She looked up and down the street. "Now what?" she thought. The voice in her head said, "No breakdowns Rosie." She walked back to the bus stop, caught the bus, and went home. For two days she sat at the dining room table staring into space. She tried to remember how she pulled herself out of the last depression. She remembered saying the words, "Help me Lord Jesus." In a voice so faint it was almost a whisper, she said, "Help me Lord Jesus."

The telephone was ringing, and she didn't realize it. By the time she came out of her trance and answered it, the phone had stopped ringing.

The next morning she got up, dressed to go to the bus stop. "Lord, please help me find something," she said out loud to herself.

The phone rang just as she had her hand on the doorknob. "Hello, is this Rosie?"

She answered yes and asked who it was.

"My name is Mrs. Blancine, and I am a friend of Mrs. Collings who you worked for. Forgive me for calling so soon after her death, but I am in need of someone to help me. She always spoke so highly of you; I didn't want someone else to hire you before me."

Mrs. Blancine's voice sounded like someone you wanted to hug. And what did she say, Mrs. Collings spoke highly of her? What? That mean old lady who never said a nice word in the thirteen months that she worked for her. "Hello, Rosie are you there?"

"Yes, yes, I'm sorry. I *am* looking for work."

In her soft, sweet voice, Mrs. Blancine told Rosie she would like her to come to her house so she could meet her. "How soon can you come?"

"I was on my way out the door to look for work. I can come today."

"Oh, that would be wonderful. If you have a pencil and paper, I'll tell you how to get to my house. Now tell me where you live." After she gave

Rosie bus directions she told her that she would reimburse her for the bus fare that she spent that day.

WOW! What kind of blessing is this lady, Rosie thought. And those thoughts continued with her on the bus ride to Mrs. Blancine's house.

Mrs. Blancine was four feet nine. She had been a widow for twenty years when Rosie walked into her house. Her house was pristine; everything in place, a speck of dust dare not land, and it smelled like bread baking. She was the direct opposite of Mrs. Collings. She smiled and grabbed Rosie's hand and shook it like they were old friends who had not seen each other for a very long time. "I am so thankful to you for coming so soon. My children say I need to stop working so hard and get some help. Please look around my house and tell me if you would be interested in helping me?"

Rosie could not believe how friendly this lady was. Her face was cheerful even when she was not smiling. She was a happy person. Mrs. Blancine invited Rosie into the kitchen for tea and homemade bread. She told Rosie what she needed her to do. "I will need you every day for the rest of this year until I get everything clean. Then we will start our spring cleaning in January. I will pay you two dollars a day more than Mrs. Collings paid you."

Mrs. Blancine was a social person. Every Wednesday she hosted a bridge party with a special lunch she prepared. She volunteered at the hospital twice a week and collected clothes from her friends for the poor. She had one daughter, one son, and four grandchildren. The four grandchildren spent every Friday night with her. Everyone called her Mommie, and she was old enough to be Rosie's mother. Eventually Rosie found herself calling her Mommie too.

The house was not large, but larger than it looked from the outside. There were four bedrooms and another room that could be a bedroom. A chauffeur sometimes stayed on site. Rosie also had her own room so she could occasionally spend the night. There was a large eat-in kitchen, a dining room, a nicely sized living room, and a room where Mommie listened to her radio programs while she knitted scarves and hats for needy people.

To say she was organized would be a gross understatement. Not only did everything have its place, it also had a special way to be in that place. The silverware was placed a certain way in the silverware drawer. Towels were folded a special way and color coordinated in the linen closet. The washcloths were folded long ways and placed on the shelf with a folded edge facing out. Each Monday all the beds were stripped and changed. If the sheets and pillowcases dried on Monday, they were pressed by the end of the day. Mommie worked with Rosie to show her how she wanted the house taken care of. But she did not overpower her. Once she showed her how a thing was to be done, she left Rosie alone to do her work.

They worked together like two friends who had known each other for years. Mommie told stories about growing up and how poor she was. Some of her stories were sad, but most of them about her childhood were fun. One day the story was so funny Rosie laughed. When she heard herself, she realized she couldn't remember a laugh coming out of her mouth for a long, long time. Laughing felt good, but she felt guilty. She believed she did not deserve to be happy. She believed God was rightfully punishing her for the *wrong she had done.*

During the third week of January, they started spring cleaning. Everything in the house had to be cleaned; everything. Every inch of wall, ceiling, floor, and woodwork was scrubbed. Every closet, drawer, back of drawer, bottom of drawer, and runner of drawers was cleaned. The silver, the china cabinet, and each piece of china was shined until every spot and speck was gone. The beds were taken apart, and everything that could be dismantled was cleaned inside out. Mommie worked with Rosie during the spring-cleaning period so that she learned the entire house and exactly how and where Mommie wanted everything. Rosie was amazed to learn that Mommie usually had done all the spring cleaning alone until Rosie came.

It took about a month to finish everything. When they were almost finished with the spring cleaning, Mommie informed Rosie that every year she went to Florida for three or four weeks in March. "The lady I usually go with is very sick. Now I know you might want to think about this, Rosie, but will you consider going with me to Florida? Of course, you will be doing me a favor, looking after me, so I will continue to pay you. I sure hope you say yes. I promise you will not have to work as hard as you have for the last month. In fact, we both need a break. You will have to help me open up the house. It has been closed up since my children were down there last summer. But after that, we will have ourselves a vacation!"

Rosie stood in the middle of the room listening to Mommie go on about Florida. She saw her mouth moving, but she could not hear her words. Her mind was racing. She was thinking about the reverend and all the trips they enjoyed together. She thought about her hard times, bad days, and depression since their split. She thought about God and how she felt she was being punished for all the wrong in her past. Then the dam broke. All the tears that she had stored in the last year came pouring out.

Mommie did not say a word. If she was shocked at the outburst, she did not show it. She put her arms around her new friend like a mother would hold a crying baby and held her until Rosie cried herself out. Rosie was crying because she felt she did not deserve good treatment from anyone. She believed that if Mommie knew her background she would not even want her to work for her. I am damned; God knows my past, she thought.

"Now, now Rosie, I know what you are crying about has more to do with your past than the present. Will you please consider the trip with me?"

The words Rosie tried to say started as a whisper and got stronger as she repeated over and over…. "You don't know, you don't know. Mommie, you are a good person, but I'm not. If you knew me; if you really knew me, you, you, you would not want me to go with you."

"I know you are kind and honest and a hell of a good worker. That's all I need to know. So will you go?" Through her sobs Rosie answered, "Yes, yes, I want to go."

Mommie had a driver take them to Florida in a spacious Packard. The drive took almost a week. They stopped often for food and bathroom breaks. There was no hurry. Mommie and the chauffeur talked a lot while they rode. Rosie sat with a long face; always looking if she were on the verge of crying. Mommie just kept the atmosphere pleasant with her stories and jokes and games. Rosie was able to stay at the same hotels as Mommie because most people thought she was white, but to be safe they ate their dinners in their room.

The home in Florida was small, but large enough. There was a pool in the backyard. Mommie had called ahead and had the utilities turned on. The furniture was covered with large white throws and everything was dusty. After they emptied their luggage, they began right away to uncover the furniture and dust. They worked like a team knowing exactly what had to be done. Before they were finished, a neighbor and friend of Mommie brought dinner for the travelers.

The next day the driver took them to the market, and they stocked the refrigerator. "There will not be a lot of cooking going on here," said Mommie, "We will eat out most days."

Rosie did not mind cooking, so on the first day she made a big dinner. Mommie changed her mind, and asked Rosie to cook every so often.

By the second week they had the house in order. The kitchen was stocked with food, the laundry was done, and it was time for a break. Mommie asked Rosie to go with her for a walk after their lunch. They walked to the beach. The sun burned, but the warmth felt therapeutic. They thought about the snow at home. Rosie had to push herself to keep up with Mommie as they walked. Everything was beautiful, the white sand, the sun, the warm breeze, the swaying palm trees, and Mommie humming as they walked.

Tears started rolling down Rosie's cheeks. Mommie asked Rosie if they were tears of joy or tears of pain.

Rosie replied, "Both. I am so happy, but I have that sad feeling that I do not deserve to be happy."

"Everyone deserves to be happy," Mommie said.

"Not a person who has done the things that I have."

Mommie put her arm around Rosie. She was so short she had to reach up to get her arm around her shoulder, "Do you want to talk about it?"

As they walked through a shady area under the palm trees, Rosie began to talk. She started with the way she connived her parents into sending her to Ballard School so she could get away from Mardine and picking cotton. She told Mommie about the rape, the pregnancy, about Blake and how she learned to love him, the short marriage and how devastated she was when Blake died. She talked about the cosmetology school, her brother coming to stay with her, working in the shop, and the nervous breakdown. Then she hesitated. The tear floodgates were open again. The words would not come out her mouth. Even though Mommie had not shown any reaction to all she had said so far, she did not feel she could tell Mommie about the reverend?

"Have you reached the part that is the hardest for you to talk about?"

"Yes." Rosie managed to get the words out with her head dropping so low her chin was on her chest.

"You do not have to tell me if you don't want to," Mommie said, with her arm still around Rosie.

"I am so ashamed of myself, " murmured Rosie. "I am ashamed for many reasons. One, because what I did was wrong, but mostly I am ashamed because that was the happiest time in my life."

They were sitting on a bench near the beach. The sun was going down and leaving behind a beautiful orange-red color. A young couple walked by who could not keep their hands off each other. They kissed and caressed all the way down the beach. Rosie was silent. Not far behind the young couple came two men who obviously had drunk way too much, and they each still had a glass of booze in their hands. They stumbled, conversing in a language understandable only to someone as inebriated as the person blubbering out the mixed-up words. The two men looked at Rosie and recognized her sadness, her red eyes, and tears.

"Ahh, I'm sorry you feel so bad. I know it must have been a man to cause all that pain." They both burst out laughing, almost spilling their drinks.

One man offered her his drink, and then the other guy grabbed it. "She can't have that; if you don't want it, give it to me."

They got into an argument right in front of Mommie and Rosie about the drink.

Mommie stood up and took control. With her little four-foot nine frame, she looked up to the six-foot men, put her hands on her hips and said, "Gentlemen, you are invading our space. Take your drinks and go away now! Can't you see we're trying to have a peaceful moment here? Your booze won't make us feel better. Be gone with you two." She shooed them both away. After looking at her in disbelief, they stumbled their way down the beach arguing about the drink.

Rosie was impressed at the little woman taking on two six-foot drunks. After the men left Mommie turned to her and said, "Now, you were saying?" As if nothing had happened. It gave Rosie the strength to tell her story.

"I had an affair with a married man. No, it's worse than that. Let me tell you the whole tale. I had an affair with a married minister."

Mommie showed no reaction.

Rosie hesitated and waited for her to be shocked and appalled. When Mommie did not react, she continued, "I justified what I was not doing because I did not have sex with him. The first time we were together he approached me and I told him no; he never tried again. I thought he respected me so much that he would not pressure me. I did not realize then that I was taking something from him, even more important than the money he spent on me–something he needed to give to his family and his church–and that was his time."

She went on to tell her about the six glorious years, the trips, the gifts, the death of the first wife, and the minister taking another wife. She told how the minister wanted everything to remain the same, but the second wife had threatened her.

With her last breath Rosie sighed, "The problem is I still love him and miss him so much, but I can't go back into that black hole. That part of my life is over."

Moments passed. There was a long silence. Finally Mommie said, "Rosie, do you believe in God?"

"Yes."

"Do you believe He forgives?"

Rosie hesitated.

"You'll not forgive until you forgive yourself. You need prayer. I'm going to ask you to go to church with me on Sunday. I've asked you before, and you've refused. Now I'm begging you."

Rosie did not answer. She sat with her face in her hands, crying, deep, heavy sobs that rose up from her gut. The sun sank below the horizon. The day was done.

CHAPTER 16

AMAZING GRACE

The choir sang "Amazing Grace," and then the minister came to the pulpit. He arranged the things on the podium in front of him. He looked around. He took a deep breath, hesitated, and looked around again. "Today I will preach about forgiveness. God loves you and God forgives you. Before he wrote Amazing Grace, John Newton had a career in slave trading. When he found the Lord and knew the Lord he asked for forgiveness for his sins. The Lord forgave him. The Lord forgave this man who worked on a ship that picked up people stolen from their home and jammed them into a space that was too small for half the people on the ship. They were underfed, and lived in inhuman conditions. Then, if they survived, they were sold into slavery.

"Our God forgave John Newton. Is there someone in your life that you need to forgive? Is there anyone here who had something happen, so bad that you felt you could never forgive the person who did it to you? Now I'm not talking about that person who bumped into you when you were walking down the street. No, no, I'm not talking about that person. Forgiving them should be easy for you. You're a Christian, right? I'm not talking about that person who gossiped about you or told a lie on you. You can forgive them, can't you? No, I'm talking about something that cut to the bone. Something that hurts to think about, that you can never, ever forgive the person for the horrible deed. You knew it then and you know it now. You have told yourself over and over that you will never forgive."

At that moment Rosie thought about Blake and what he did to her in that cemetery when he was supposed to be walking her home from school.

She thought how she fought to keep her clothes on and how he pulled her panties down and raped her. She thought about how much she hated him. She thought about how she eventually forgave him and learned to love him.

"Some of you have something in your background that you can relate to what I am saying." The minister seemed to look right at Rosie. "You might say to yourself, what kind of God would let something so bad happen and then expect me to FORGIVE? Ha, forgive?" His voice went up another octave.

"Well, I am here to tell you that our God is that kind of God. I am here to tell you that our God expects you to forgive others just as He forgives you. There is someone here who is holding something in their mind."

Rosie felt his eyes on her again.

"There is someone here who has something they are holding on to. Something you have done that you feel God cannot forgive." At this point Rosie was sure Mommie had talked to the Minister. Then she realized that Mommie had been with her ever since their walk and her confession the night before.

"Now if you think you have never done anything that you need to ask God for forgiveness for, I'm telling you right now, you need to wake up, look up, and pray up. You and I are not perfect. You are no better than I, and I am no better than you. Look around the church, there is not a person here who has not fallen short of God's expectations. Why do you think he sent His Son to die on the cross? Why do we call Him our Savior?

"When you pray the Lord's Prayer, listen to the part *'Forgive us our debts as we forgive our debtors.'* Yes, forgive us our debts, because we do not even know what all we owe. And while you're asking the Lord to help you forgive others, and while you're asking the Lord to forgive you for the sins you committed, ask for one more thing. Ask the Lord: The Lord who has forgiven you for your sins! The Lord who has forgiven others for sins trespassed against you. The Lord who loves and forgives you. Ask that same Lord to help you forgive yourself, "Lord help me forgive me." Know that our Lord has already forgiven you, and now you need to forgive yourself. Amazing Grace. Yes, it is amazing."

The words rang in Rosie's head like a clanging bell.

"Ask the Lord to help you forgive yourself. We ask Him to help us forgive for the things we did to others. Now, while you are down on your knees, ask Him to help you forgive you for what you did to you. Ask Him to help you forgive you for the things you did that you wished you had not. Ask Him to forgive you for the thrill, the joy, the happiness that you felt when you were sinning. Ask Him to forgive you for enjoying the sin. Ask Him to clean your mind, your heart, and your actions. Pray and then pray some more. When you finish, pray more.

"Do you think he will help you? Do you think He sees what you are doing or have done and decided you are not worth saving? Then you do not know my God. You don't know the God who through Jesus talked to the woman at the well who had many husbands and the one she was with now was not her own. Read about that in your spare time. You don't know my God who loved David even though he knew a woman and then had her husband killed so he could marry her. Look that up in your Bible. You don't know my God who put up with whining, complaining Israelites and brought them to a land flowing with milk and honey. He forgave them.

"God wants to hear from you. Talk to Him. Listen to Him. Stop hating, whining, and sinning. God has asked us to, first. Love Him with all our mind and all our soul and obey Him. Then God asked us to love our neighbor as we love ourselves. Please turn to the page in your Bible where it says love only the neighbors who have not done anything to make you angry. Raise your hand when you find that page. And while you are at it, find the page where it says I should love only the neighbors who look and act just like me. Then turn to the page that says not to love the neighbor who is a drunkard, the killer, the prisoner. Don't we know they have enough problems to work out without adding our hatred? They sure need our prayers. God has forgiven them, and He forgives you.

"People, you are all here today for a reason. I don't have control over who comes and does not come to church on any given Sunday, but God does. It is not a coincidence that I preached this sermon on this day. God tells me what to pray, and I listen to him and do his will. So, if you heard something that touched a sore spot with you...KNOW that God is trying to get your attention....LISTEN!"

The rest of the sermon was lost to Rosie. She heard and remembered only the word, *forgive.* As they walked quietly home from church that day Rosie finally said, "I have some work to do, don't I?"

Mommie didn't answer. She knew Rosie would work it out.

The vacation in Florida improved after the first church visit. After that, Rosie and Mommie went to church every Sunday. Rosie's long face started to turn the other way. She found herself laughing and talking. She even told Mommie some of the fun stories about her childhood. They laughed, they ate, and they enjoyed the vacation.

The trip home was more enjoyable than the trip down to Florida. The three of them sang songs and talked all the way home.

For the next two years Mommie and Rosie were like two sisters. Rosie looked forward to going to work to spend time with her boss who was also a friend. She ceased thinking of her job as a job. Although Mommie was busy with her charity work, they still found time to catch up and visit while Rosie did her work. When she left on Friday she was looking forward to Monday.

Every Saturday Cousin Gladys came to get her hair done. She was always full of family and friends' gossip. Rosie could tell she was bubbling to tell her something, so she tried to avert the catty gossip by talking about her working family. Something was always happening with those kids.

"You won't believe what Bobby's costume was for Halloween!" Rosie talked real fast so Gladys could not get a word in any way.

"So, they all wanted to make their own costumes. Anne used sheets and curtains for her princess costume. Will was a pirate with a big patch over one eye. Sally dressed up in her dad's shirt and hat. Then Bobby came down with a cape and a tee shirt with the letters LERT written on the front. Everyone looked at him and asked him, 'What's a LERT?' On cue, he jumped back with a totally surprised look on his face and said, 'This is ALERT.'

"We laughed so hard. Every time I think of it I get so tickled."

Rosie had to sit down because she was laughing so hard. When she looked at Gladys's blank face and realized Gladys didn't get it, she laughed even harder. By the time she stopped laughing, Gladys was still looking at her like she was crazy. "Don't you get it, Gladys? A-LERT!"

Gladys was not trying to get it. She had something she wanted to tell

Rosie and Rosie was all excited about a Halloween costume with LERT on it. "I don't get it and I don't get why this is so funny to you."

"Rosie," Gladys said, "I want to tell you something. Obviously, there was no getting around what she wanted to say. Rosie put the curlers back on the gas stove, wiped her laughing tears, and waited for the gossip.

"Rosie, do you know the reverend is real sick? He might be dying."

Rosie started curling the back of the head from top to bottom. Her hands were moving fast making the curlers click, click, click. She did not comment.

Gladys continued, "And his wife bad-mouths him to everyone."

Rosie tried to interrupt, "Gladys, that part of my life is over and….."

Gladys went on, "His wife won't take care of him. They say he's living in squalor. Some people are saying he's getting what he deserves."

Rosie took the curlers from the fire and sat down.

"Gladys, I have tried to put that part of my life behind me. I know God has forgiven me for being sinful. I am sorry for what's happening with him now. He took care of me for six years and I want to tell you a secret; Reverend was wrong spending so much money and time on me, but I will always hold him in esteem for never insisting that I have sex with him. He respected me."

Gladys' voice went up octaves, "Respected you? Rosie, don't you know? You think it was because he respected YOU?"

Rosie looked at Gladys and was puzzled. "What are you trying to say?"

Gladys's head dropped, "Rosie, he was impotent. He couldn't have had sex with you if he wanted to on his best day if God had allowed him to."

Rosie let out a gasp like a helium balloon flying backward around the room.

Gladys continued, "You were one of his trophies. It wasn't your body he wanted; it was your beauty. He and his other cronies tried to outdo each other when they gathered. You weren't the only beautiful woman he showed off. He had a small harem. Those ministers paraded their women around like Vashti in the Bible. They were brought out to show off the goods. It's what they did."

What little respect Rosie had held onto for the reverend evaporated. Her magic carpet no longer flew.

Monday when Rosie went back to work she found Mommie still in bed. She said she started feeling dizzy after church. She had not called any family because she wanted to wait until Rosie got there. "They're all so busy, I hate to bother them."

Rosie scolded her, "As much as your family loves you, they are going to be very upset that you did not get in touch with someone." Rosie went right to the phone and called Jennifer knowing she would contact the rest of the family and call the doctor. That day Mommie was admitted to the hospital with a slight stroke.

The family asked Rosie to continue to come every day to keep Mommie's house in order and to visit her. Rosie would take the bus to Mommie's house and do her general cleaning. At noon someone would take her to the hospital, and she would have lunch with Mommie. Mommie would try to be her cheerful self, but Rosie could tell she was getting weaker. The left side of her body was still paralyzed after two weeks.

On a bus ride home Rosie started thinking, What's next? Would Mommie ever go back to her home? Should she start looking for another job? JOB…that word didn't fit her life with Mommie, but she had to do what she had to do. What if she had another boss like Mrs. Collings? Dreadful thoughts ran through her head. Rosie wondered if she could take care of Mommie, but she knew the family would want the best care possible for Mommie.

The next day Jennifer was at the house when Rosie got there. Seeing her gave Rosie that sick feeling in her gut. It could only be bad news. She had reached the end of the rainbow. Two years of a job that paid her enough to pay her expenses and have some left over and a job that she enjoyed; now was it over?

Jennifer guided Rosie to the kitchen table and told her to sit down. Rosie was afraid the news was worse than she imagined. Was Mommie dead?

Jennifer started, "Rosie, the family had a meeting last night and we're going to have to make some changes. We're concerned about Mommie's health, and we feel she can no longer live alone, even if she does recover somewhat. She'll probably never fully recover. William and I've to build her a mother-in-law suite in our house so she'll be close and family will be with her at all times. It'll take about three months to get the unit built and Mommie moved in."

Rosie was holding back the tears. She knew they had no choice but to do what is best for the one they loved so much. She understood, but she already felt abandoned without her friend Mommie to see every day. She wondered how much longer they would need her. How soon would she have to start her search for a new job? She realized she was no longer listening to Jennifer, just worrying about her own future.

"Rosie," Jennifer said and brought her out of her thoughts, "we need your help. First, I want to ask you if you'd be willing to work for me and my family? I know it'll be a handful with four children and a sick senior, but we'll have additional help. We need you because Mommie needs you, and we love you like family. When we build her suite, we'll also have a bedroom for you.

"Mommie will be in the hospital for a while. We want to close up her house, pack all her belongings, and send them to our house. Of course, we have to talk this over with her. Is it possible for you to work with us closing her house? Someone will be with you half a day almost every day, but most of it you will have to do by yourself. I know this is a lot of information for you to take in at one time. Think it over a couple of days, then we'll talk again. Please continue to come every day just like you have. Mommie would miss you if you didn't visit. I think she looks forward to seeing you more than her own children."

Jennifer had given her a lot to think about. The best part was it was all good. Could she handle working with Jennifer and four kids every day? What would be expected of her? She enjoyed the kids, but now they were only at Mommie's once a week, but every day?

"Lord, Lord what am I to do?" She prayed aloud.

That week flew by, but Jennifer and Will wasted no time with the construction plans. Within two weeks they had an architect and a contractor. By the end of the month construction had started. At the end of the second month, they were painting and putting in carpeting. The addition was one large room with two bedrooms and a small kitchen. Each bedroom had its own bathroom. The large room had a bay window with a window seat and a gas fireplace under the small mantle piece. When finished the room was bright and cheerful. Jennifer bought furniture and though she didn't need help, she asked Rosie's opinion about the decorations.

CHAPTER 17

THE BUCHANNANS

Will and Jennifer had five children, two girls and three boys. The oldest was Anne, named after her mother Jennifer. She was the little mother of all her brothers and sister. She sometimes answered their questions when the real mother asked them something. She dressed them and fed them, talked baby-talk to them, and cried when someone scolded them. They all listened to her like she was their second mommy.

The second child, Will, was named after his father William. Will was a builder. From the time he got his first set of blocks, he started building things. He would stack anything to make buildings, bridges, towers, and houses. He used blocks, chairs, pillows, and tables to make his buildings.

Sally liked books. She liked to write, color, and read books. There were times when Anne would have Sally read to Bobby and Will while Will built his cities. The covers and pages of the Little Golden Books, which Mommie had given the children, showed signs of hard use by little hands. Jennifer read to them over and over so much that Sally had memorized the pictures and could tell the story just like her mother.

Bobby, the baby of the clan, was easy going. Everybody loved him. He could play or not play, read, listen to the radio, or just sit by himself and think. He was ready to join any games if asked and didn't care if he weren't asked. He saw both sides of most situations and became the mediator in arguments.

Finally, the addition was finished and Mommie moved in. The family asked Rosie to spend the night the first few nights until everyone had adjusted. The four children visited Mommie in her new room as soon as they got home from school. They all crowded around Mommie, each wanting her attention more than the other–except Bobby. He stood back and waited his turn. After making sure Mommie had everything she needed, Rosie sat down on the floor and gave them all her consideration.

"Well don't you all look sharp today?"

Before she could ask another question, Anne told her why everyone was wearing what they were wearing. "Sally doesn't like to wear long stockings, but she has to wear them anyway. Sometimes she takes them off when she gets home because our mother does not want us to play in our school clothes. As soon as we make sure Mommie is alright, we have to change our clothes. You don't have to stay here if you don't want to. We will make sure Mommie has everything. Last night she asked me for some water, and I got it. I made Will check on her last night before we went to bed to see if she wanted anything else. The nurse was here, but I wanted to be sure she was OK."

"You know, Anne, I want to do all I can to help Mommie while I am here, but I think I am going to need some help. Do you think you could be in charge of helping me while I stay here? You know how to take care of Mommie much better than I do. Maybe Sally, Will, and Bobby can help sometimes, too. It's too bad they can't talk because I wanted to ask them something."

"Oh, they can talk, but they don't want to right now. I know what they want to say, so I talk for them. What did you want to ask them?"

"I wanted to ask them what happened with them today, but if they can't answer I'll just ask you and when you tell me." Taking a piece of candy from her pocket, she said, "I'll give you this candy."

The other three did not say a word. But they licked their lips and moved closer to Rosie and Anne. They looked at Anne with pleading eyes as if to say, "Let us talk so we can get some of that candy."

Anne took the hint and asked, "Do you have more candy in your pocket?"

Rosie took out three more pieces of candy.

"Tell Rosie what you did in school today." The other three started talking all together.

"No, no, one at a time. Will, you go first."

When they finished Rosie gave them all candy and thanked them for sharing their day with her. Jennifer came into the room and sent them to change their clothes and do their homework. Rosie thanked Anne for helping her so much.

"I see I can count on you." Anne swelled up with pride and led her siblings to the other side of the house.

"That's quite a young lady you have there," Rosie complimented Jennifer. "She's ready to take over whenever you need a break1"

Jennifer and Mommie laughed knowing what a control person Anne was.

Helping Rosie up off the floor, Jennifer asked, "Is your room suitable? Did you find everything you need? How did everything go on your first day in your new place?"

"Everything is wonderful. Thanks so much for the new pajamas, slippers and robe in my room. How did you know I liked pajamas instead of a gown? I never wear a gown, you know. And if we don't like everything, it's our own fault. You involved Mommie and me in everything."

Rosie asked Jennifer to come into her bedroom; she wanted to show her something. "We'll be right back, Mommie," she said over her shoulder.

When they were in the room she asked Jennifer if she was okay.

"You seemed a little stressed. Has this move been too much for you? Is there anything I can do to help you?"

Jennifer's tears fell before she could say anything. She dropped her head in her hands and began to sob. "I'm crying and I should be happy. Our business is growing so fast William can't keep up. I'm trying to help him, but with four young children I'm going in circles. I need good people around me that I can trust. Rosie, I need you so much. I want to make you a proposition. I will hire someone to do the deep cleaning and someone to help Mommie, but if you will help with the cooking and the children, I can help William with the company. Some of the work I can do at home, but sometimes I have to be at the factory. I need someone here. Of course, I will pay you more."

"Whew," gasped Rosie, "that's a lot to take in all at one time. Let me think about this."

Before she could answer, Will ran into the room crying and holding his arm that looked broken, followed by Anne who calmly announced,

"Will needs hospital care. Rosie, will you stay with us while Mother takes Will to the hospital?"

Rosie worked four and a half days a week. She went home early on Friday. The Buchannan family did everything to make her life enjoyable. They brought her gifts and gave her bonuses. The kids loved her. She spent a good part of the time on the floor playing games or reading books. They loved her cooking and after she learned their favorite food she could easily build a meal.

Each morning when Rosie came to work, the two little people would welcome her with a big hug like they hadn't seen her in months. She would take the kids into Mommie's room, and they would all have breakfast together. After lunch and story time she put Sally and Bobby in her bed for a nap. Rosie would wake them just before Anne and Will came home from school. By that time, she had finished preparing dinner. They would all go to Mommie's room for afterschool snacks and juice. Mommie, Rosie, Bobby, and Sally would listen intently to all the things that happened at school each day. The older kids would do their homework while Rosie read to Sally and Bobby.

When Jennifer came home, she and the children would drive Rosie to the bus stop. They would not leave until the bus came. They didn't want Rosie to be lonely, even though there might be a dozen other people there.

Rosie was the surrogate mother to the Buchannan children. The days passed, then the months, and then the years. The children grew. Rosie was there for the ups-and-downs of growing children. She took care of the children and of Mommie.

Then one day Mommie closed her eyes and died. After Rosie fixed dinner she came back into the room to wake Sally and Bobby. She looked at Mommie and thought she looked so peaceful. When she got closer, she realized she wasn't breathing. It was a blessing that Jennifer was home that day. Rosie was afraid to be near dead bodies. She held her piece until she summoned Jennifer, then she took the kids into the other side of the house until the ambulance came and took Mommie away.

The funeral had a calming effect on everyone. The minister knew Mommie although she had not been to church for two years because of her condition. He frequently came to the house to pray and give her communion. The Buchannan family had Rosie sit with the family. Some people wondered who and why she was there; the family knew that Rosie was as much a part of the family as the blood relatives.

After the funeral Anne came to Rosie and put her arm around her and cried. "Rosie, what happens to all the parts of Mommie?" Rosie tried to explain that the body went into the ground and eventually disintegrated.

"No, I'm not talking about the body, I know about that. I mean the parts of Mommie that I love so much, like the warmth in her smile and the look she gave me showing how much she cared for me. I saw that look when she looked at you too, Rosie. The feeling in her arms and hands when she touched you like a grandmother. The pain she felt when I was in pain. And when I was in the room with her, I knew she was there because I would just feel her presence. The draw she had that made us want to be around her all the time. I could feel that. What happens to all that stuff?"

"Well, Anne, I believe that's the part of us that goes back to God. That stuff or those parts are called love. Love comes from God and when we are finished with it we pass some on to others, and the rest God gives to someone else. **Remember, it's only love when you give it away.**"

"God gave you some, Rosie," Anne said as she put her arms around Rosie's waist. "You have some of Mommie's love. Maybe God is in charge of giving love, but I think Mommie gave you some of hers, too. I hope I got some of Mommie's love to give to others. I want to have a lot of love to give."

"Anne, I think you have a head start on most people your age. You give love when you take care of your sister and brothers. You keep doing that, you will give more love away than Mommie ever had."

Anne gave Rosie a big hug. "I love you, Rosie." She felt better.

George called from the army base to tell his mother he was getting out of the army. "Don't worry Mom, I have a job. My buddy had me take the Post Office test and they sent the results to Detroit. I'll start work two months after I get home.

A month after George got home he got his own apartment. Rosie helped him furnish and stock up. He still came to her house two days a week for dinner. Rosie would cook at the Buchannans and then come home to cook for George. She babied him just like she did before he went to the army. She washed and ironed his clothes. Every other week she cleaned his apartment. Every time she saw him, she told him it was time for him to start looking for a wife. Taking care of three houses was taking its toll on her, but her house was the only one that suffered.

One Sunday George called her to say he was bringing a lady friend to dinner. Rosie was impressed with the tall, beautiful, young lady he brought home. The only problem Rosie had with the soft-spoken lady was that her name was Roxie. (Later, Rosie would ask him if he liked only women named Roxie.)

Rosie took a liking to this Roxie right away. After dinner, Roxie insisted on helping with the dishes. Rosie was shocked when George helped too. George just wanted to be near Roxie–he could not keep his hands off her. Every time Rosie went back into the dining room George backed Roxie into a corner.

The next Saturday Rosie spent her morning washing, ironing, and cleaning. Gladys would come today, and after Rosie finished her hair, she would take her to the store and then to George's to drop off his clothes. When Gladys asked how George was doing Rosie sounded a little concerned. She had not heard from George all week. He brought his dirty clothes when he came to dinner with Roxie on Sunday, but she had not seen or heard from him since.

After she washed, straightened, and curled Gladys' hair, Rosie loaded George's clothes in the car. When they got to his apartment, Rosie saw his car parked out front. Maybe he was sick– that's why she hadn't heard from him. Rosie told Gladys to pull up close to the door. "I'll be right back." She had a key, so she let herself in. The room smelled like cigarettes and alcohol. She heard voices. When she got inside the door, she saw George having sex on the couch in the middle of the front room with the curtains open.

"Oh my God! George can't you and Roxie have a little respect for each other. If you're going to mess around like this, close the curtains and get married?"

The woman under George was not Roxie. Her head popped up and she yelled at Rose, "Roxie? Who the hell is Roxie?"

George grabbed his underwear and threw the woman his undershirt, as she yelled, "Who is this woman, George? Does your damn cleaning lady just walk in without even knocking? " The woman stood up and the undershirt fell on the floor. Rosie shook her head in disgust, dropped the clean clothes on the floor, turned, and walked out. She heard the woman still cursing as she went out the door.

Rosie closed the door just in time to stop Gladys who was headed to the apartment. Gladys could see that Rosie was upset.

"What's the matter?" Rosie was crying now. "Just when I thought he had got himself …..sob… sob.. together…..sob….sob…Roxie is such a nice girl… ." Gladys didn't ask, but she sure wanted to know what went on in that house. When they got to the store Rosie sat in the car a minute to get herself together before she could go in.

George came over that evening to apologize to his mother.

"You don't understand. I'm a man, I have needs."

"If you have so many needs, get married. What's wrong with Roxie?"

"Roxie is nice, but there's something. I can't put my finger on what's holding me back from asking her. Mom, I do love her, but I am scared of a commitment with her."

"George, if you love her and she loves you, MARRY HER!"

They talked all evening. George still had his doubts about Roxie. "Son, there is no perfect woman. God knows you are not a perfect man. The perfect woman sure ain't that thing you were with this morning. Is that the kind of woman you would want to be the mother of your children? Can't you picture yourself with Roxie for the rest of your life?"

"Sure, the Roxie you saw is wonderful, but sometimes there's another Roxie that comes out all moody—solemn and depressed."

"I think you're just hard on her because she won't lower herself to that… that… other woman's standards. You need to think about this George before you get someone pregnant. Pray, Pray, Pray."

George did not come to dinner Sunday. Rosie was afraid that he was with that loose woman again. She called him on Wednesday but didn't get an answer. She would not go to his house again without checking with him first. The week passed. She was beginning to worry. On Friday when she got home, she saw George's car in front of her house. She opened the door to see George and Roxie standing there, smiling.

OK, what's up with you two? You look like the cat that swallowed the canary. Together, Roxie and George yelled, "We got married."

Life was easier at home because Roxie took care of George, his clothes, and his apartment. They still came for Sunday dinner. Rosie was happy for them, and they seemed happy with each other. She wished life at the Buchannan house was as easy.

Life at the Buchannans had become stressful. Jennifer was coming home later and later. When she got home, she was exhausted. William got home after Jennifer and the children were in bed and got up early and left for work. One day Jennifer came home early. Rosie told her to sit down; she needed to talk to her. Jennifer feared Rosie was about to tell her she was quitting. Or was it something bad about the kids? By the time Rosie opened her mouth to speak Jennifer had run a bunch of scenarios through her mind and none of them were good.

Rosie pulled a chair up to the table and took Jennifer's hand, "What's going on?"

Jennifer looked at her confused. "What's going on where? What do you mean?"

"I'm going to paint a picture. Tell me if you recognize anyone in it. The wife and husband are working too hard. The mother comes home late. By the time dinner is over she is exhausted, and the kids have to go to bed. They don't spend any time with their mother. The father is a ghost in his own house. Laughter and fun have disappeared. The husband and wife do not have time for the kids and no time for each other. Notice I'm using all dark colors in this painting."

Jennifer interrupted, "The company is growing in leaps and bounds. We had to hire new people, get new machines, learn to operate the machines, and then train everyone else! William is working 16 to 18 hours a day. We only talk to each other at work. I feel more like his co-worker than his wife. I should be happy, but I am stressed out, tired, and sad. I don't know how to laugh anymore."

"I don't know the answers for your workplace," Rosie admitted. "But you two have to do something about your home life or you will see this beautiful family fall apart. You two can work this out, but first you have to realize there is a problem. Is your company more important than your family?"

"We are building the company for the family. It is taking longer to get off the ground than we both thought. In the long run we're sure it will pay off."

"Jennifer," Rosie spoke slowly, "When was the last time you and William went out on a date?"

"A date?" Jennifer's voice rose. "I forgot the meaning of that word. Our company needs us twenty-four hours a day. We love each other and we love our kids. We are doing what we have to do for each other and the family. We don't like working so hard, but there is no other way right now."

Rosie let Jennifer defend her and Will's actions. She let her talk until Jennifer was hoarse. She stopped talking and looked at Rosie blankly. And then with growing awareness, she whispered, "I'm trying to convince myself, aren't I?"

"I'm glad you finally heard yourself. I was wondering how long it would take. Now listen to me." Rosie was talking to Jennifer just as she was sure Mommie would have talked to her if she were alive. It was firm but loving.

"You've told me many reasons why you have to spend time to keep your business afloat. Do you have that many reasons to make a family happy? Those kids don't give a hoot if your company makes it or not. They see you and William barely speaking to each other. They miss the fun and laughter in this house. They miss their parents. Now, I've been thinking of solutions. First, you need to talk to your husband so you're both on the same page. I'm sure once you talk to Will, he'll realize, too, that you have to come to the middle. What do you say if every Thursday I spend the night so you and Will can go out together, alone? This is a start. I believe if you two start spending time with each other you'll find time to spend time with your children. What do you think?"

This worked for years —until Kate and Blake came to live with Rosie.

CHAPTER 18

KATE AND BLAKE

Nine-pound Blake Lawrence Maxwell came into the world looking up with large eyes to see his father, mother, and grandparents staring down on him. George insisted that his first child must be named after his father who had left him in charge of the house. Blake was a beautiful, butterball of a baby with a head full of black curly hair. He brought joy to everyone. He started smiling when he was less than a month old, and it was a smile that never faded. Rosie never tired of him. He was the answer to a grandmother's prayers.

Although George wanted to name his second baby after his mother, Roxie won the argument. She named her after her favorite sister, Catherine. Soon after Kate was born, Roxie went into a deep depression. George could not deal with the problems that Roxie was having, so he took the children to Roxie's mother, and he lived the life of a single man. Many nights he didn't make it home long before it was time to go to work, smelling like smoke and alcohol. Eventually Roxie started drinking and the children spent more time with the grandparents than with their parents.

The telephone rang while Rosie was curling Gladys's hair. It was Roxie's mother calling to see if Rosie could keep the children for the weekend. She asked Rosie if she knew that Roxie had been sick, and the kids had been staying with her for the whole week. Rosie did not know. She asked what the problem was with Roxie. The mother could not exactly identify the problem. She knew that Roxie was confused and slept a lot. She told Rosie she thought it was a good idea to get the children out of the house for their own sake.

Rosie asked her what George was doing to help.

"We haven't seen George in two weeks," she said shortly. "The kids and Roxie have been here with me."

Rosie had Gladys take her and pick up her grandchildren. She was so disappointed with George she did not even try to call him. She called Jennifer and told her she would have to bring her grandchildren to work with her on Monday.

"I'll explain when I get there."

By Friday, George had not called or come to the house to see about his children. Rosie called a neighbor to watch Blake and Kate. She got a cab and went to George's apartment. She saw his car in front of the house. She knocked on the door, but no one answered. Finally, she went to the building superintendent, telling him she was George's mother and asked him to open the door because she felt something was wrong.

The superintendent answered, "Yes, something is wrong. I hear yelling, fighting and things breaking up here all the time. You can be sure I am going to get them out of here as soon as I can." He took out the large ring of keys and fumbled around until he had the right key.

Rosie's mouth dropped when he opened the door. The apartment was strewn with trash. Furniture was turned over and broken. All around were empty whiskey bottles, beer bottles, broken glass, cigarette butts, and ashes. The smell of garbage was strong. She heard snoring and was afraid to look in the bedroom. She asked the superintendent to wait while she walked into the room and called George. The snoring continued. She called louder; the snoring continued in the same rhythm.

She found George and Roxie asleep. Trying to wake them, Rosie yelled, but they snored as if synchronized. Rosie looked around the bedroom. Cigarette butts, dishes, and even though the children had been gone for over a week, she saw dirty diapers, brown and crusty. Rosie had to watch her step as she walked through the rooms. The superintendent shook his head.

When George woke up he smelled something that was familiar to him: his mother's cooking. For a minute he did not know where he was. He looked around the room. The room was in order—everything except the bed where he and Roxie were. Roxie lay there beside him snoring loudly.

Her breath smelled like she may have puked; then he saw puke in the bed and on him. He didn't know if he had puked on her or her on him.

He knew his mother was here or had been here. He looked around for a window to climb out to escape the looks and reprimand she would give him. He tried to get up but his head pounded so that he fell back on the bed. Slowly he managed to rise and make his way to the bathroom. The smell of food was making him sick. He didn't want his mother to hear him throwing up. Before that thought slipped out, he was throwing up in a bathroom that Rosie had cleaned about an hour before.

She must have been here all day, he thought, as he threw up again. He needed a cigarette and a drink. He was sure that was the only thing that would stop the throbbing in his head. He had a bottle in the kitchen. Before he went to bed he always made sure to have a bottle to wake up with. The problem was, the bottle–and his mother–were in the kitchen.

He tried to squeeze some toothpaste out of a tube that was already flat. He washed his face, and stumbled into the bedroom looking for something clean to wear. Now he was getting mad. He was not mad at himself for the mess around him, but mad at his mother. He was thinking that he should not have to answer to her. *I'm a grown man. I can do whatever I want to do. She ain't got no business in my house. Didn't I tell her that the last time she burst in unannounced? How did she get in anyway? This is my apartment. Where is that pack of cigarettes? I wish she would take that smelly food out of here.*

Just then his stomach growled. He could not remember the last time he had a decent meal. "Damnit, I need a drink."

He kept arguing with himself unaware that he was talking out loud. Roxie woke up and slurred something about the food cooking. She stumbled half-dressed to the bathroom bumping into George as she passed by him. She smelled terrible.

George could hear his mother in the kitchen. He wondered out loud if he could get out the door and down to the bar to get a drink without her seeing him. Rosie had cleaned up the mess in the living room. Yet, George was so hungover that he stumbled and fell over furniture that had been returned to its rightful place.

Rosie heard him and came out of the kitchen. She ran to help him up.

"Quit helping me...leave me alone.... go away...". Then crying like a baby, he stumbled around and went to the bar for a drink.

During the next week Rosie kept her grandchildren, and neither George nor Roxie called to see about them. Rosie tried to call them, but she never got an answer. During the weeks that followed they were shifted back and forth between Roxie's family and Rosie.

Rosie went to work depressed, stressed, and tired. Jennifer was now concerned about Rosie. "OK, it's my turn to have a talk with you," she told Rosie. "Tell me what is going on."

Rosie told her about George and the kids. She was worried about them being shifted between families. She told Jennifer she did not know what to do.

"George needs help, I can't help him, but I have to see after my grandchildren. I don't know what to do." Jennifer and Rosie sat at the kitchen table and worked out a plan for Rosie to take care of her grandchildren and work. Rosie called Roxie's mother and asked if she could keep the children on Monday and Tuesday; she agreed. Rosie would not work on Wednesday and then on Thursday she would take them with her to Jennifer's home. They would stay until Saturday morning.

George and Roxie eventually separated. Roxie had good days and bad days. George continued to drink, but not as much. He came for Sunday dinner and sometimes he brought a girlfriend with him. Rosie was never impressed because she knew the next time there would be someone different.

When Blake started school Rosie took him to a neighbor's house in the morning before she went to work. The neighbor would send him to school and be there when he got home. Rosie had a routine. Everything was going smoothly.

Then, George got a new girlfriend. After a short courtship he moved into her large apartment. Betty fell in love with George's children and wanted George to keep his own children. Rosie had no say. George told her he was going to take them, and there was nothing she could do. Six months later he and Betty broke up. George brought the children back to Rosie.

"That is the last time you are going to shift these children around," she told him. "If you take them again, I'm going to the police and have you arrested. These kids do not deserve what you are doing to them. Please get your life together."

Blake and Betty reunited, eventually married, and bought a two-family house where Rosie and the children could stay with them.

Rosie moved in. . . under protest. But she lived there for years.

CHAPTER 19

ROSIE'S BIRTHDAY PARTY

Jennifer and her children filled the room. It was their idea to bring dinner and cake to Mrs. Smith's home, where Rosie was now staying. This was going to be a celebration. Kate had thought that only some would come, but they all came, including some of the grandchildren.

She welcomed everyone, "I'm so happy that so many of you are here to celebrate my grandmother's 90th birthday. This is as much a surprise for me as it is for her."

Kate walked over to her grandmother and put her arm around her. Rosie did not acknowledge her hug. She continued to smile and rock back and forth in the large chair.

"Kate," Bobby spoke quickly and emotionally, "We all want to thank you for taking such good care of your grandmother. You know, she was our grandmother too. We know you had your hands full, raising three boys, helping your husband with his medical practice, being a homemaker, and taking care of your grandmother with Alzheimer's—and her dog! We thank you because we love her so much. She helped us all through some hard times."

"No, stop right there, whoa....I have to say this loud and clear. I will never, ever be able to do as much for my grandmother as she did for me and Blake. I don't do nearly as much for her as she did for us." Kate was starting to choke up. The words would not come out of her mouth. "Let me tell you my story."

"Before Blake and I started school, Momma Rose took over guardianship of us. Not legally—no one paid her to do it, she just did it.

My parents didn't ask her to keep us; that was her decision. She was almost 50 years old when she took on the task of raising two small children under the age of five. You guys remember when she brought us to work with her? She did whatever she had to do to keep us together and happy."

"When our father married his second wife, they bought a house and Daddy insisted we move into the upstairs apartment. This was right after she stopped working for your mother," Kate looked in Will and Anne's direction.

"It was probably the best thing for all of us because since Momma Rose didn't drive, Daddy helped her a lot. The house was in a better neighborhood. Momma Rose didn't want to move, because she knew longevity was not a strong suit with my father and his women. But we went with them, and it was a good move. Somewhere around my teenage years we had this cute newspaper boy who lived around the corner. He became good friends with Blake. My dad always said that newspaper boy didn't fool him. He was using Blake to get to me. My friends who lived on the street were children of doctors and lawyers. Momma Rose saw that they had more than we did so she took on a part-time job to buy new furniture so that I wouldn't be embarrassed when my friends came over. She always bought good clothes for me and Blake. I heard her say often that her grandchildren would look as good as the doctors' and lawyers' kids."

Well, Rich and I started going together; he graduated from high school and went to college. He asked me to wait on him until he got a degree. Momma Rose insisted that I go to college even though we really could not afford it. I know she got some assistance from the Buchannan family."

She looked around at all the brothers and sisters. "Well after he graduated, we got married, once again even though we could not afford it, we had a nice wedding. I bet your family helped to pay for that too. Rich decided to be a doctor so he went back to school. I worked, had a baby, then another. I don't know how we could have made it without Momma Rose. She bought clothes for the boys, made dinners for us, and sent money regularly. She even babysat so Rich and I could go out.

Right after my third son was born, my dad died. Momma Rose wanted to die too. She loved him so much. She went into a depression, not eating or sleeping. She lost a lot of weight. There were times when she would pass out because she was so weak. Rich had just started his internship in Toledo. We had to move. The house we could afford in Toledo didn't allow dogs. We'd just bought a dog for the boys. We asked Momma Rose to keep the dog until we found someone who wanted him. As fate would have it, she fell in love with that little schnauzer. He became her life. She needed someone to take care of, and Snapper filled the bill. He would come up to her and put his paws on her knees and talk to her and she would talk to him.

'You want a dog bone, Snapper? Is that what you want? You know you can have whatever you want. Yes, you can, yes you can.'

"Many times, we heard her say, 'Nobody loves me but Snapper.' Then she would start looking for him. 'Where are you, Snapper?' Then Snapper would appear and look in her eyes and show his love.

"The Alzheimer's was sneaky. We noticed she would ask us the same question over and over. Then those same questions started coming closer and closer together. She would tell us stories, the same stories over and over again. She would have the same story, the same voice tone, and the same hand gestures. We just thought it was a condition from getting old.

"Rich and I moved to Alabama and my cousin drove her down for a visit. He told us this story when he got to our house:

'In the beginning of the trip, we got into the rural area. Auntie (my cousin's name for Momma Rose) looked around and saw a corn field, "Look, do you see that field of corn? My father was a farmer. He had a lot of acres. He grew cotton. My sisters, brothers, and I helped him pick the cotton. Then one year the boll weevil came and wiped out the whole crop." He added, "When she said 'wiped out' she waved her hand to show everything that was wiped out."

'Wow, that must have been devastating.

'She answered, 'Yes, it was.

'Then she sat quietly as if thinking of the sad event. Driving along the highway we came to another cornfield, and she said, "Look, do you see the field of corn? My father was a farmer, he had a lot of acres. He grew cotton. My sisters, brothers, and I helped him pick the cotton.

Then one year the boll weevil came and wiped out the whole crop."

'She waved her hand the same way as she did the first time she told the story.

'Wow, that must have been devastating.

'She answered, 'Yes, it was.'

'After that, I tried to distract her if I saw a field of corn ahead. If she saw it, I heard the story again. A couple of times she went to sleep but would wake up just as we came to the cornfield.

'By the end of the trip, I hated corn and cotton. Needless to say, it was a very long trip.'

"Eventually, Momma Rose moved in with our family. We didn't know how serious her condition was. We had her examined, but we still thought she would be OK. Eventually, she started to wander away from the house. Neighbors would find her and bring her home. As her condition worsened, she didn't know who we were. She thought we were holding her prisoner. She would call relatives and ask them to come get her. She asked someone to call that girl she used to take care of who married a doctor. Someone told us about Mrs. Smith and this assisted living home. Everything has worked out fine. Momma Rose seems to be happy here. We didn't know that Mrs. Smith would love her as much as we do. She takes care of her like she is her baby."

Mrs. Smith was standing beside Rosie. You could see the love in her eyes, "Mrs. Maxwell is easy to take care of. Sometimes she's alert and knows what's going on. Then there are times when she's completely disoriented. She has a very good appetite and most nights she sleeps eight to ten hours. There was a lady here who was 102 years old. From the first day Rosie walked in the door, Cora adopted her like she was her caretaker. Cora helped Rosie get dressed. She took Rosie to the table and would feed her if she wasn't eating. Often, the two of them would come down the hall hand in hand.

"Well, we lost Cora right before her 103rd birthday. At first, Rosie looked for her. She asked about Cora constantly. We didn't know if we should tell her right away. One day she asked, 'Where is Cora?' We told her Cora had died. Rosie said, 'Why did she die?'

'Rosie, Cora was almost 103 years old.'

Mrs. Smith wound up the punch line of her story, 'Rosie gave me a mean look and said, 'So what? She didn't have to die.'"

Everyone laughed.

Mrs. Smith said, "I'll tell you something else about Mrs. Maxwell. She is a charming, loving, sweet senior citizen, but because of her Alzheimer's condition we don't give her enough credit for her awareness. Mrs. Maxwell was complaining to us about the man with the red coat and hat outside her window. We thought it was a figment of her imagination. She insisted that he was out there. I looked out the window often just to reassure her no one was there. All of us tried to convince her that no one was outside her window, but she insisted."

Kate said, "Oh, you heard about him too. She told me about him the last time I was here. I looked out the window, but I didn't see anybody."

"Well, the other morning the aide was changing Mrs. Maxwell's bed. She reached across the bed to pick up a pillow that had fallen on the window side of the bed. And there he was. He was around the corner a little, but she saw him—the man with the red hat and coat. You could only see him if your head was on the pillow. Mrs. Maxwell was absolutely right. We owe her an apology."

Everyone looked confused. "Who is he? What is he doing outside her window? What's going on?"

Mrs. Smith laughed. "I'll answer the 'what' first. He is helping protect this building. He's been there for many years. Who? He is our very own red fire plug. If you look out her window from her viewpoint, you can see the red hat and the arms stretching out like a little man. Everyone laughed. So, to make her happy, we planted a bush to block *his* view from her window. From now on he will be named the "peeping plug.""

After dinner and cake everyone went into the large room with Rosie. She seemed to know something special was happening. Some awareness started to penetrate the shell that surrounded her brain. Her four surrogate children, two grandchildren, and Mrs. Smith were all here. She looked around the room trying to absorb each face, each person. She smiled and rocked back and forth, occasionally clapping her hands as if she just saw something special.

Each person in the room wanted to sit next to Rosie. Kate looked around the room at Jennifer and her children. She asked a question that made everyone stop and think, "I know you all love her a lot and she loves each of you, but there seems to be something more in your relationship with my grandmother. I can see it when you look at her and when you kiss and hug her."

The room became exceptionally quiet. Everyone was looking off in space.

"Alright, I'll start," Bobby began, "Since I am the youngest and, of course, the cutest."

A roar went through the room.

"Rosie and I had a pretty good relationship until that day we went to the store."

Everyone started to laugh remembering the incident.

"All of us went to the store with Rosie whenever she had to go to the store. She wouldn't leave anyone home alone.

"When we were walking home, I lagged behind so no one would see me reach in my pocket and eat the candy that I took from the store. Rosie had eyes in the back of her head, because she spun around just as I got a mouthful.

"'Bobby, what are you eating?' I started to stutter, cry, and pee all at the same time. Rosie stared me down and asked again what I was eating. I couldn't swallow and I was afraid to spit it out. My sisters and brothers were oohing and ahhing over the pee making a puddle around my feet. Rosie's voice got a little louder, 'Bobby, where did you get that candy? If you can explain yourself, we'll go home, but do **not** add a lie to the wrong you have already done. I am waiting.'

"I told her I picked it up while we were waiting in line.

"'Did you pay for it?

"I don't have any money, I cried

"'Bobby, in this world if you want something, you pay for it in one way or another.'

She turned us all around. I was making wet footprints in my own pee. She marched us back to the store and asked to see the manager. When the manager appeared she told him that I had taken candy without paying for it. She asked him what I could do to make up for the two cents that I owed him. The manager gave me a very mean look. I think I peed again. 'Young boy, you will have to bag groceries for five minutes, OR GO TO JAIL!' I didn't see the wink that he gave Rosie. I stood there with the puddle at my feet and the wet spot on my pants and bagged groceries like the man told me. I cried all the way home.

"I hated Rosie that day. As I grew up I remembered that embarrassment and never stole another thing in my life. I don't even cheat on my income taxes. She taught me to be honest, and I appreciate that. We laughed about that after I got older.

"She helped me over another really rough spot in my life. You all know now that I am gay. When I was young, I didn't know what was wrong with me. I didn't want a girlfriend like my friends. Yeah, I played along like I had a girlfriend, because Sherry chased me until I agreed to go steady. I didn't have any feelings for her. I didn't want to go to the Prom. Rosie asked me one day if I was excited about graduation and the Prom. I told her that I really didn't want to go. She asked me why. That's when I told her I didn't like girls like that. She listened. She listened when I told her that I was more attracted to Sherry's brother than to her.

"Rosie didn't react like I thought she would. She asked me to talk to Mom and Dad. I didn't want to. She told me I might have a situation that Dad could help with. I was afraid if anyone knew that I was different they wouldn't like me. Rosie told me there are all kinds of people in the world. If you look at anyone you can find something different about them. She asked me if I could be comfortable with who I was. We talked for over an hour. She convinced me that I should hold my head up and live my life. She convinced me to talk to Mom and Dad, but I really believe my talk with her helped me get over that hurdle in my life. Like Popeye, 'I yam what I yam.'"

Someone shouted out, "And we all love you!"

Anne said, "I thought you were going to tell about the time you put sunflower seeds up your nose because you wanted your friends to think your boogers had shells on them. Rosie had to get them out with the tweezers."

Kate hadn't heard about that one and she couldn't stop laughing.

"Well, you think your stories were a love-hate, mine was bad." Will had to speak up to make himself heard over the laughter.

"When I started middle school, I had a new group of friends. I was trying to fit in and be like them. The good part was they were a smart group of guys. They were all honor roll students. I had to work real hard to keep up. Most of their families had money. The school had an assistant janitor who happened to be a man of color. One day, as the guys sat around at lunch, they started talking about him. All the things they said about black people were mean and nasty. Our family never talked about other races. We never saw any black people. I didn't know, at that time, that Rosie was black. She looked just like us.

"One day we were in the park. I had just reminded Rosie to be sure to come to the school when I gave my speech. She usually came whenever we won awards or gave a presentation. She said she was looking forward to seeing me perform. Just then we saw a black family with their kids. This was a rare sighting. I said some ugly things about them—things I'd learned from my new friends. I thought what I said was so funny.

"Rosie grabbed my arm and looked me in the eye. 'Where did you get that ugly talk from? Do you think everyone who is different from you is not as good as you?

"I gave her a smart-mouth answer, 'No, just the black people. White people are better than black people.

"'Why?' Rosie asked.

"'Because we are smarter, and they are dumb.

"'Do you think I am dumb?

"'No, just black people.

"'I'm black,' Rosie said.

"I'm sure I changed as many colors in those next few minutes to be legally classified a rainbow. I didn't believe her. 'No! You're not black.

"'Yes, I am. Everyone you see who looks white is not white. Many people even claim to be white, and they are not. You may be black.

"I started to cry. I hollered, 'I am not black and I hate you. You tricked my family. I'm going to tell my mother and father that you're black! And I don't want you coming to my speech.' I ran home crying to tell Mom what Rosie said."

Bobbie cleared his throat and added, "I'm ashamed of that time now. I apologized and Rosie and I made up. She knew I loved her. But, you know, as I grew up, I realized how some white people perceive black people. I notice sometimes when I'm with a group of white people and they tell a story with a black person in the story, even if it has no relevance to the outcome of the story, they mention the race. And when they say black, if a black person is there, they say, 'Blaacck,' like it's a bad word or it's going to offend. I'm not perfect; I still have a lot to learn about race relations, but I thank Rosie for showing me people are people. There are good and bad in all races."

Jennifer had been sitting quietly all evening. Now she had something to say. She talked very softly so everyone was very quiet to hear what she was saying, "Everyone here has their own special reason for loving Rosie. Now I am going to tell you another reason why all of you, and I, should be grateful to her.

"When Rosie first came to work for us after Mommie had a stroke, our company was just beginning to grow. Your Dad and I were working extra hard to make the business a success. It got to a point where we rarely saw each other except at work. Our home life was a mess. Rosie recognized that we had become co-workers and not husband and wife. She made herself available to us so we could have a date night. I'm sure this saved our marriage. If it hadn't been for her, well, . . . I don't want to think where we all might be now. The last years of William's life were better because we learned how to love each other–because of Rosie."

"Mom, tell them what you told people when they asked you why you didn't have a boyfriend after Daddy died."

"Oh, I always say, I do have a boyfriend. He's short, bald, no teeth, still lives with his parents, is younger than I am, doesn't have a job or a car, and can't drive. After I enjoy the shocked look of the questioner, I say that my boyfriend is my grandson!

Laughter filled the room.

A young girl came into the room asking if anyone wanted coffee. She filled the cups and left the room.

Anne said, "Well, my story will come as a shock to you all. Remember my first year when I went away to school?"

Everyone looked down as if they were picking lint off their sleeves.

"It was my first time away from home and I met a football player who paid me a lot of attention. I was in love. He wooed me... He told me he loved me....I had sex with him. He told me I could not get pregnant if it was my first time. I believed everything he said."

She paused to let everyone ingest the words she said. "I got pregnant. He dumped me when I told him. I told my best friend. She told me to get an abortion. She knew someone in our town who would do it. I didn't have the money and I didn't know who to ask for any. When I came home I asked Rosie to lend me money. She wanted to know what I wanted it for. I wouldn't tell her. She asked if I was in some kind of trouble. I started crying so she patted me and hugged me and asked me again what I needed the money for.

"Finally, I told her I was pregnant and I was going to get an abortion. She asked me if I'd talked to Mom. I told her I couldn't. Rosie told me to let her think about the loan for a day and she would give me an answer the next day. I was anxious waiting for her to come to work the next day. She put me off until all of you and Mom were gone. First, she hugged me and let me cry in her arms. When I had gathered myself, she began to talk.

"Rosie said, 'Right now, you probably feel that you have let everyone down. I know you're ashamed of yourself. Now we have to talk about the best thing for you and the life growing inside you.

"Those words shook me up. I hadn't thought about a life growing inside me.

"'I'm going to ask you to rethink your plans for an abortion,' Rosie said. 'You've made one mistake, please don't make another. By killing the life you've made, you'll dwell on it for the rest of your life. That is a serious thing. I want you to think of this plan. If you agree to put your baby up for adoption, I have a friend who lives way out in the country. You can go there for your summer, have the baby and go back to college. No one has to know, except...except you have to tell your parents.'"

The room was quiet.

"I kept sobbing. Rosie said, 'Think this over, Anne. We can talk about it tomorrow.' I went to my room and sat staring at the walls for hours. I heard Mom when she came home, I heard all of you. I heard Rosie leave.

"That evening after everyone had gone to bed, I went to Mom and Dad's room and told them everything. I don't know what I was expecting them to do, but it wasn't what they did. They both got out of bed and hugged me. I apologized for letting them down. Dad said, 'Apology accepted,' and they hugged me again. I told them I had talked to Rosie, and she insisted I talk to them. I told them I wanted to get an abortion. I thought I could do it without telling you two. We all cried.

"The next day Mom talked to Rosie. When you guys thought I went to school all summer I was sixty miles away having a baby whom I gave up for adoption. I know you all are shocked and ashamed of me."

The brothers and sisters were all silent.

"Say something!" Anne pleaded.

Finally, Bobby spoke up. "We all knew."

Anne's mouth gaped open. She shot a look at her mom.

"Mom didn't tell us. OK? Nobody told us, we were just nosy enough to find out on our own. We found a letter from you to Mom and Dad. We all agreed we would never mention it unless you did."

Anne lowered her head and shook it with hands over her eyes. "You knew? You all knew? You knew all these years, and no one ever said anything to me?"

All heads were nodding.

"Well, did you know this? Two years ago, I started looking for my daughter and, last year, I found her!"

Now, this revelation shocked everyone. Mouths flew open and eyes bugged. "What! And you didn't tell us?" they hollered

"I wanted to see how everything went. And I wanted to tell all of you at once. We talked a couple of times and then I met her. She looks just like us. She wants to meet all of you."

The siblings were all happy and dancing around. "When can we meet her? Where does she live?"

"Oh I'm so happy this is out in the open. Let me go to the restroom and I'll be right back and fill you in on everything."

"No, hold that pee and tell us now."

Anne was laughing and crying as she left the room. The room buzzed with the news of their new niece.

Anne came back with the girl who had earlier brought in the snacks. "Everyone, meet Joy, your niece."

Screams, cries, and hugs….

Joy walked through the crowd and went right to Rosie. "I'm so happy to formally meet all of you. I've thanked Rosie many times for saving my life. She is a blessing to me. I loved her before I ever met her. I'm so happy to be here with you. I wanted to meet you as soon as my mother told me about you.

"With the help of God, I have this lady to thank for my life. Many young girls have been in my Mom's position and made other decisions they felt were right at the time. I can't condemn them, but I can say, 'Thank you, God,' for leading my mother to Rosie. She saved my life."

The box of tissues went around the room. Anne had to take more than one. Then, she asked her sisters and brothers, " I was wondering if you would get the hint from the flowers. A yellow rose for love and baby's breath, *Love, Joy*…get it?"

They all howled again.

Rosie had sat through all the dialogue. Everyone chatted and fussed over Joy. Rosie suddenly stood and walked over to her. She put one hand on each cheek. Her face was very close to Joy's. She smiled at the girl with a new mother's smile, filled with love. All the chatter stopped because everyone was watching Rosie.

A light came into her eyes. A beautifully calm smile covered her face. In a small voice she said to Joy, "I loved **you** then." She spoke clearly so everyone knew what she said, then she turned around and sat down.

Very softly, she said, "I am finished."

The light in her eyes went out.

It took some people longer to leave than it took them to get home. Many thought this was the last time they would see Rosie. She smiled as they hugged and kissed her and told her goodbye over and over. Finally, the party was over, and Mrs. Smith was able to get Rosie to bed.

A week later Mrs. Smith went into Rosie's room to wake her for breakfast. Rosie was cold. Her hands were across her chest in a praying position. She had slipped away.

Joy asked Kate if she could buy the gown for the funeral. Kate agreed.

As the hundreds of mourners passed by the casket, they looked down at a beautiful woman. Her face was smoothed into a peaceful expression and she was wearing the most beautiful BLUE DRESS.

---THE END---

EPILOGUE

By the author

I came to know Rosie as "Auntie" because she was my husband's aunt. She lived upstairs in the two-family home with her grandchildren, Kate and Blake. She did most of the cooking and it was so good. She also took care of her grown-up son, George, who lived downstairs with his wife. Auntie cleaned the house until she taught her grandchildren to help her.

When Auntie visited her friends' homes, they had to make her sit down and rest. She always wanted to help everyone. In the evenings she and her friends played cards, and she was so good. She usually won most of the games and they were shocked if she did not win. And there were surprises; she would often bring out a big hidden cake to end the day.

In the summer she would come to our house in the country and visit for a week or so. When I got home from work, the cupboards would be cleaned, dinners would be made, and the dog would be walked. Before she would leave to go home, I would always tell her all my problems, and then Fred would tell all his.

Over the years, after losing her son to cancer and after the grandchildren moved out to live their lives, she was alone at home. Auntie did not like living alone, especially in Detroit. She did not drive so she had to get someone to drive her to the store, doctor, or church. One of her nephews told her he had a house in Cleveland that he would rent to her. She agreed and they moved her in. When she got there she did not like it. The kitchen was on the first floor and she was on the second. She would hear loud talking downstairs. She thought someone was stealing from her. She felt the darkness in the light. She did not know the people in the house next door. She was mixed up and confused—REALLY CONFUSED.

She got in touch with her grandson who had just retired from the Army and moved to California. She asked him if she could stay with him. He agreed and the family helped her move. Unfortunately, the living situation in California was not good for Auntie. A friend found out and contacted her granddaughter, Kate. Not long after, Kate brought Auntie to her home in Alabama.

At this point, Auntie's Alzheimer's was getting worse. She began to believe her granddaughter and her husband were mistreating her and she wanted to get away from them. Auntie often called friends and family to tell them she was being abused and wanted to get away. Days went on and she and Kate's family were not getting along well. Kate's husband told her she needed to send Auntie to a nursing home. He was afraid that someone was going to get hurt. Eventually, they found a pleasant, safe place where a few nice seniors lived and took her there.

At first she did not like it. But, a little bit later she was in the game. The lady in charge of the nursing home was very nice and helped Auntie a lot. There was also a really short lady there who took Auntie's hand and walked her around and showed her everything. In a short time, they were all friends. Her short friend showed her how to get up, get dressed, go to breakfast, lunch, and dinner. The short lady was with her all day. They got along so well and were always together. The two didn't talk too much but they knew how to stay together.

At her high age of 90, Rosie's family decided to give her a birthday party that frames the story you read.

A WORD FROM THE AUTHOR

I started this book by listening to my favorite relative. She lived through many good days in her life, but she also experienced some extremely painful years. She wanted to get her story out of her mind, so I listened. Year after year during my visits to her home in Detroit, I simply listened as she shared more and more about her amazing life. I started writing down her stories and eventually stitched them together into the book you're reading now.

Some parts of this story are a bit hard to read. Other parts will make you laugh and some might bring a few tears. But I hope you'll see this is a story about hope, courage, love, and endurance.

I want to thank my nephew, Danny Brown, for taking the time to read my story and pass it on to my son, Ricky Brown. I want to thank both my nephew and son for not giving up on me and helping me get this story to the point where I can share it with the world. I want to thank my daughter, Terri Brown Ford, for her help in marketing the book. I want to thank the rest of my family for your interest and support, and I ask for your grace and open minds as you read about family members you know and love. (Their lives were sometimes difficult, but they were always guided by love.)

Finally, I want to thank anyone who had enough interest in this story to pick up this book. More than anything, I just want people to enjoy and learn from it.

ABOUT THE AUTHOR: AMY BROWN

Amy (Perrin) Brown was born and raised in Cleveland Ohio. She married Frederick Brown on February 21, 1963. It wasn't long before Fred took Amy to visit his aunt in Detroit. During those visits, "Auntie" began telling her stories, and Amy began listening.

Amy has two adult children, Frederick "Ricky" Brown, Jr., currently in Dallas, Texas, and Terri Ford, who resides in Euclid, Ohio with her son, and Amy's grandson, Ray Patrick Ford III. Amy is also a sister, aunt, and great aunt to dozens of nieces and nephews, and friend to countless others in her church and community. Anyone who knows Amy well is used to hearing her ask, "How can I help?"

Amy currently resides in Mayfield Heights, Ohio, which keeps her close to her daughter and grandson. She's also been known to hop in the car or on a plane to visit her son and granddog in Dallas. When she's home, her favorite pastime is quilting or playing a game of Words With Friends.

This is Amy's second book. In 2004, she wrote *Laughter Over the Hill - Nursing Humor, Smiles, Hints, and Hugs* after spending many days in the nursing home as a volunteer.

Made in United States
North Haven, CT
20 January 2023

31369591R00093